Praise for *Room Temperature:*

"A major cosmic drama . . . It is a delightful book . . . *Room Temperature* is a real charmer, a breath of fresh air, a show-stopping coloratura aria made up of the quirks of memory and the quiddities of daily life."　　　　　*—Sacramento Union*

"As bold and original as Baker's first novel . . . but the truth is, I think *Room Temperature* is better. It is sweeter, more poignant; therefore braver."　　　　　*—Mademoiselle*

"*Room Temperature* will deliver a welcome warmth . . . This is a small masterpiece by an extraordinarily gifted young writer."
—Publishers Weekly

"Nicholson Baker displays the same abundant observational skills he showed in *The Mezzanine*. Here, however, he adds a subtle dimension of warmth."　　　*—Cleveland Plain Dealer*

"Intensely funny and moving."　　　　　*—Entertainment Weekly*

"It's wonderful."　　　　　*—San Jose Mercury-News*

"Stunningly original . . . rich in playful humor, and with an abundance of ingeniously observed detail."　　*—Library Journal*

ALSO BY NICHOLSON BAKER

FICTION

THE MEZZANINE

U AND I

VOX

THE FERMATA

THE SIZE OF THOUGHTS

THE EVERLASTING STORY OF NORY

THE ANTHOLOGIST

A BOX OF MATCHES

CHECKPOINT

NON FICTION

HUMAN SMOKE

DOUBLE FOLD

THE SIZE OF THOUGHTS

THE WORLD ON SUNDAY

ROOM

TEMPERATURE

R O O M

TEMPERATURE

A NOVEL

NICHOLSON BAKER

GROVE PRESS
New York

Originally published in 1990 in hardcover by
Grove Weidenfeld, New York.

Chapter 1 and parts of Chapters 3 and 4
first appeared in *The New Yorker.*

Printed in the United States of America
Published simultaneously in Canada

ISBN-13: 978-0-8021-4491-1

Grove Press
an imprint of Grove/Atlantic, Inc.
841 Broadway
New York, NY 10003

Distributed by Publishers Group West

www.groveatlantic.com

10 11 12 13 14   10 9 8 7 6 5 4 3 2 1

For Alice

I placed a jar in Tennessee . . .

WALLACE STEVENS

R O O M

TEMPERATURE

1

I WAS IN THE ROCKING CHAIR giving our six-month-old Bug her late afternoon bottle. Patty was at work. I had pulled the windowshades halfway down: sunlight turned their stiff fabric the luminous deep-fat-fried color of a glazed doughnut. Still visible from a year earlier was the faint outline in adhesive of one of the lengths of masking tape that we had Xed excitedly over the windowpanes before a hurricane that hadn't panned out; below it, a metal tube of antifungal ointment lay on the sill, its wrinkled tail spiraled back like a scorpion's, its Scotch-taped pharmaceutical torso of typed information so bathed in light now that I could make out only the normally pedestrian but now freshly exotic name of the prescribing pediatrician, "Dr. Momtaz." The shade-pulls, rings wound apparently with common kite string, lunetted pieces of the distant horizon for further study: a section of a water tower, a brilliant white sweat sock of steam that was slowly emerging from one of three smokestacks across the water some-where in Charlestown, and a rotating bun-shaped air vent on the top of a twelve-story old-folks home in North Quincy, whose dents and irregularities sent corpuscles of pewtery dazzlement in my direction. Half a mile away, some dark birds, not gulls or crows I don't think, were on their way toward Boston. Their flight reminded me strongly of something, and as they flapped slowly from the sky under one windowshade to the sky under the next, I realized that the movement of their wings as they turned this way and that, negotiating big chunks of wind, was remarkably similar to the flapping of a small dog's ears as it ran at full speed in excited zigzags across a field. I was extremely pleased that the sight of several silent far-off birds could remind me of the yapping frolicsomeness of a puppy—it seemed a tricky lateral sort of comparison, in which the two terms threaten to be insufficiently disparate in some respects for the connection to work properly, as if you said that the sun was in some way or other like the moon. Other birds, much farther away, rested stilly against the haze like flakes of ground pepper. The whole outside, in fact, what I could see of it, looked unusually good and deserving of similes today—cleaner, sharper, more richly colored: I had removed the screens from the windows the day before, because the hot weather seemed to be gone for the year.

Also as a result of the weather, I was wearing a sweater for the first time in months, one Patty had given me for my birthday: a brown monster stout with various fugal inversions and augmentations of the standard cable knit, and consequently glutted with insulational dead air, its corona of lighter outer fibers frizzing out three-eighths of an inch or more from the slubbed and satisfyingly clutchable weave that formed the actual structure underneath, so that the sweater, along with me, its wearer, appeared to fade without a demonstrable outer boundary into the rest of the room, as tuning forks or rubber bands will seem in their blurred vibration to transform their material selves into the invisible sound they generate; a machine-made sweater, but manufactured apparently with Xenakian lurches and indecisions programmed into the numerically controlled needles that, unlike the chain flayings and bleaching stains used in production lines to antique new furniture, gave it to my eye an attraction distinct from the irregular grandmotherly alternations between close attention and indignant abandonment at historical preservation meetings prominent in handmade knitwear. Patty had ordered it for me from a catalog; when I shifted my weight slightly in the rocker, the sweater's mute woolly bulk made me feel particularly fatherly and head-of-householdish—though in fact it was Patty, working three days a week at an advertising firm to my two as a technical writer for a medical imaging company, who got us health insurance. I was pleased to see how comfortable the Bug looked with her head in the crook of my arm, unaware through the loft of all that yarn of my elbow tendon tautly supporting her.

Like a screech trumpet player, she held her bottle with one hand; her other hand roved in search of textures: my sweater's, of course, but also a wrinkle and the nipply bump of a snap on her own striped outfit, her hair and ear, and especially the raised ounce and cubic-centimeter demarcations that were molded into her Evenflo bottle's plastic, like the fractions of a cup that had once been molded into glass peanut butter jars, so useful for practicing your fingertip-reading skills on while you ate. The raised outlines of the peanut butter jars' "$1/3$"s and "$3/4$"s would act, I recalled, as lenses, focusing light, projecting secondary cashmere images (not shadows) of themselves through the thickness of glass and onto the browner inner cylinder of the peanut butter, images that were often easier to read than the molded markings themselves, which were only partially defined by high-lights. My mother told my sister and me that when she was breastfeeding us she ate peanut butter straight from the jar with a tablespoon, and perhaps because of her own maternal craving she didn't mind later when I took a full jar and a silver spoon upstairs with me while building my plastic models. (I "chopped" models by gluing out-of-scale chrome-plated halves of engine blocks and exhaust systems from funny cars and dragsters onto the wings of warplanes.) The taste of the peanut butter was sharp enough to make my eyes water, and the glottally claustrophobic sense of being repeatedly on the verge of choking on several overlarge gouges was appealingly risky, although I sometimes preferred rather to work a single spoonful down very slowly, setting it aside on the newspaper for a moment when I needed two hands (in order, for example, to detach one half of a ram-air induction scoop from the molded parking-lot grid of engine components to which it was linked by twisting it back and forth until the plastic finally whitened and gave way); each time I withdrew the spoonful from my mouth, my upper lip left a freshly aerodynamic shape on it that sharpened my already fierce appreciation of the plane's swept-back airfoils and cockpit canopy. And when I had finished hybridizing the model—when the last McPherson strut was glued prominently to the side of a jet nacelle, where its ornamental usefulness was not lost, as it was when hidden in the uninteresting stock car's body whose components I was using— the remnant of peanut butter in the back of my mouth allowed me to simulate more convincingly the fricative roar of a rib-crushingly tight turn on the test flight above the *Golden Encyclopedia*; and this in turn contributed to my sense of the fitness of the name Skippy: *k* sounds came very naturally to the mouth during and after a major spoonful. And then, eighteen or so years later, not long after Patty's urine pinkened conclusively in the plastic vial, she asked me if I could maybe pick up a small jar of peanut butter on my way home from work. Absolutely! Before that day, I had never heard her express even a mild interest in peanut butter. I'd stopped eating it myself. I jabbed a tablespoon vertically into the new six-ounce jar I had chosen for her and left the arrangement in the middle of the kitchen table for her to find when she got out of her shower; and then I thought better of this over-preparation and pulled the spoon out and smoothed out its C-shaped intrusion and tightened the lid again so that she might think that the seal had never been broken, because she might want (as I certainly had wanted years before) the pleasure of being the first to dig into the lunar surface herself. She probably would want to use a knife and make a sandwich anyway, I thought. I put the spoon in the sink. But half an hour later I found her flipping through an in-flight magazine with the jar open on the arm of the couch and a teaspoon upside down in her mouth. Tears came to my eyes. "Straight from the *jar*, baby!" I said. Soon she had a stomach profile as smoothly Bernoullian as my model-building Skippy spoonfuls, and I, perhaps influenced by that anecdote in Shakespeare about the votaress who got pregnant and grew, like a sail, "big-bellied with the wanton wind," began to visualize her lying with her legs strapped down in a wind tunnel wearing a shiny leotard, giving teasing effleurage to her dome, calling for a technician to apply some Chap Stick to her lips from time to time, while I, a promising young engineer at work on the next generation of airbus wings, evaluated the inexplicable magnitude of lift her Bug-mound aroused in the moaning tunnel's air by pumping luminous gases through the smoke rake and watching

7

their streaklines veer upward and interlace, laminarity disrupted by the brief fuss of her pubic hair, shedding into elaborate lasso shapes and beehives of induced flow that after only a few minutes of flight-speed wind made the entire research installation knock and shiver with worrisome resonances.

2

It was three-fifteen on a Wednesday. I had been singing "Over Hill, Over Dale" over and over to the Bug, gradually letting the consonants dull into a continuous vowely whisper, inhaling some phrases and exhaling others, and I had been rocking and rocking. The *Times Literary Supplement* was open on my knees to a long review by Grevel Lindop of Coleridge's marginalia, but I had lost interest in it, and though my knees flexed and unflexed, I had the paper adjusted so that it was quiet. And surprisingly, I seemed to have rocked my way to a rare stretch of floor and angle of attack that resulted in a nearly silent ride. I sat near the bookcase, where we normally gave the Bug her bottle, but instead of the floor's usual contributions—the nail-shank knuckle-pops, the load-bearing grunts, the Curly "nyuck-nyucks" and the crow-barrings of polite inquiry that in forward and backward sequence made up a unique rhythmic bar code for every possible permutation of rocker placement, compass bearing, center of gravity, and level of humidity that could arise in the room—instead of this considerable racket, which seemed not to affect the Bug and didn't

9

bother me most of the time, although occasionally I would have fits of indignation that made me think of Schopenhauer's fury at the idle cracking of buggy whips by coachmen on his street, there was at the moment no floor noise at all: which meant that nothing could distract the Bug and me from the pleasurable experience of the irregular topography of the floor itself as it was conveyed mutely and sleep-inducingly up through the chair to our bodies. Perhaps it was this lumpily tangible chiasmus, rather than simple back-and-forth oscillation, that made the rocking of babies so effective. It was like riding a slow train. On each backward transit there was, after a few small jostles, a much more substantial squeakless joltlet that made the Bug's head jog slightly against my arm, wobbling her bottle—and I was pleased to imagine the caressive rounding and dulling of that abrupt eighth-inch drop from one floorboard to another by the wood's slight give, by the stretch in the cane seat and the deformability of my bottom, by the pillowiness of my sweater, and by the resilient shock-absorbency of the lovably paired muscles in the nape of the Bug's own neck, until it had become something that helped put her to sleep. It was the old princess-and-the-pea thought, the question of how many mattresses it would take to oblige some discontinuity to the point where it would fail to register: something I used to consider whenever I rode a bicycle down a newly paved side street and ran over one of those black rubber air hoses that traffic engineers used to leave across one lane, leading to a small green box in which every tire that passed was recorded on some sort of internal sphygmograph, along with the time of day, so that they could apply complex formulas that were probably stolen from telephonic queue theory developed by people at Bell Labs in order to arrive at the proper intervals for red and green lights at the nearby intersection, whose old green-painted four-sided traffic light was being replaced with a cluster of four yellow-painted individually hung traffic lights on aluminum poles, with buttons that infrequent pedestrians could press to suspend the ideal timing with a walk sign. Was I, on my bicycle, on rubber tires that were filled to a higher pressure but which bore a lighter weight than a car's tires, counted by those data hoses? Had I thrown off the calculations affecting key residential intersections all over southeast Rochester, New York, by seeking out those hoses and bicycling over them dozens of times, and once even getting off my bike and jumping repeatedly on the sensor to ensure that a particular traffic light's green cycle would be unusually long, because it was on the way home from my friend Jim Heydemann's house? What power I had!

Now, of course, traffic engineers were less quantitative than they had been then: the reduction of complex volitional and social processes such as residential traffic to mathematical models had come under attack, and the potentially greater subtlety of non-mathematical acts of judgment based simply on years of driving indignantly around was widely conceded—probably the extra crossings I had contributed no longer influenced the green and red intervals today. Or was I wrong about that? It might be, simply because the interstate highway system was long completed and the excitement had seeped away from much of civil engineering, that as the theorists and theory admirers moved on or retired, their duties were inherited by uninspired and indifferent functionaries, rather than by subtler empiricists and connoisseurs of automotive impatience, and that as a result some of the old formulaically arrived-at intervals put in place when the signal boxes were first programmed still persisted, reinstated simply by rote after any repair job or modernization, so that my many spurious bicycle-crossings still affected the orderly flow of traffic down East Avenue in Rochester, even as I sat rocking my daughter to sleep on Wollaston Hill in Quincy, Massachusetts, over twenty years later. I had counted for something in that town! But it was just as likely that the hoses had not even registered my weight: after all, the similar red rubber hoses that lay near the pumps in gas stations in those years, back when every station had an air machine, didn't; car tires made them ding every time, but only if you had just pumped up your bike's tires, and you dipped hard with your knees at precisely the right moment as you crossed the hose with the rear tire, lifting the front in a near wheelie, could you sometimes set the dinger off with a bicycle tire—and even then the repairmen in the garage were never deceived: sometimes they didn't even look up from their idle adjustments, or they looked up with dull hostility, because they knew that dings from cars came in pairs.

3

ACROSS THE ROOM, above the white crib, hung a mobile that Patty had made in the early weeks of the Bug's life. It turned slightly, though the air seemed still, and the sideways text of one of its pale-colored pendants came into view:

ARMHOLE PRESSING

NO. 11

The previous fall, with Patty's help, I had bought a new tweed jacket to wear to work, and in its normally useless outer breast pocket I had found, soon after becoming a father (while stuffing into it a number of Slim Jim spicy smoked snacks that I planned to hand out at the office in place of the standard cigars), a handful of these inspection slips, which were a little wider than fortune-cookie fortunes but had some of the same flimsy, touching portentousness: whispers from beyond the known world of the discount retail outlet, direct from the production line. BLOCKING NO. 4. LABELING NO. 5. Earlier suit jackets of mine had offered similar sacraments of quality control, and each time I had been pleased to discover them, sometimes after wearing the jacket for years without any need for the particular out-of-the-way pocket they waited in: but I had always smiled at them for a moment and then regretfully thrown them away.

This time, though, their faded colors held me—the cheek tint of LAPEL NO. 3 and the urban-horizon blue of IMPRESSION NO. 5 and especially the near celadon of LINING PRESS NO. 13. Two of them said: "If any defect should be discovered / Return this ticket with garment." The use of the subjunctive argued for manufacture in a place that once had been under British colonial rule, I thought; on the other hand, communications of this kind had a strangely international epidemiology, their style diffused through the demimonde of packaging copywriters and printers and uneasy technical people who wanted their language to free itself of all messy contingency and rise into the timeless sphere of pure procedural abstraction. (You could see, for instance, the artificial laconicism suddenly grip the mock-elegant copy on boxes of fancy frozen vegetables: though there was plenty of room for untelegraphic commands, the style would abruptly shift from the fluting of "Tender baby peas picked at the point of perfection and gently simmered in fresh tarragon butter and then quick frozen to seal in" etc., to the field-phone brusqueness of "Place pouch in saucepan. Bring to boil.")

Holding the sheaf of inspection slips like a bouquet of dried flowers, I went into the kitchen, where Patty had a breast flipped out feeding the Bug for the second time that day, and I said, "Look what I found in my jacket pocket, Honey-honker! These are much too beautiful to throw away!" I put them down in a fan next to a neat pile of nursing pads, and when I got home from work Patty was halfway through making a mobile out of them, hanging them sideways by white threads from various lengths of plastic straws so that they balanced in tiers. She'd saved them! She'd made permanent use of them! And she told me that as she had worked on the structure she had had an idea for a mail-order product: the customer would send in his family tree, and its configuration of marriages and progeny would be built into a mobile, each generation represented by a tastefully graduated shade—or, if that product proved too labor-intensive to make money, we might offer a do-it-yourself family-tree mobile kit, for older kids, that had telescoping crossbars and tags and Magic Markers for filling in the names of each relative.

I told her she should write these ideas down, because she had similarly promising ones like this fairly often (for instance, a coffee-table book of yachts' interior designs), but she didn't: she had begun writing in a spiral notebook every night, but I gathered that it was mostly observations about the newborn Bug. I would bring her her glass of water and get in bed while she sat against her pillow with her knees up, and I would stare from inches away at the lamplit overlapping-squares pattern of her flannel pajama bottoms (why didn't the ink with which the pattern was printed ruin the fluffiness of the flannel's nap?) and try to "read" by ear what Bug-events she had found noteworthy that day. I wanted, as a first step, to isolate some simple word, like "sleep" or "milk," from the complicated sequences of felt-tipped sniffing sounds her pen made. I wasn't successful. Sometimes if I cranked my eyeball to its limit I could see, over the diagonal of one side of her open notebook, the top of her pen whirling in its tight little epicycles, and with that visual supplement to the sound, I think I possibly decoded the aural image of the word "nipple." Or was it "happy"? Was this skill even within the range of human ability? The only TV show my father ever got excited about was *Secret Agent*, and

15

once, when we all were watching, Patrick McGoohan made a stethoscopic tape-recording through a door of a man dialing a phone number (on a dial phone, of course) and then moments later, at another telephone, re-created the phone number by a spellbindingly heuristic fingerstroke-by-fingerstroke matching of the dial-rewind times he had taped. But McGoohan was distinguishing between ten possible numbers on a telephone dial—I, in listening to my wife's diary-writing, was trying to distinguish between twenty-six letters, plus the occasional capital, and spaces and punctuation. You would know that it had been a *t* you had heard and not an *i* at the end of the word only when the grapheme was dotted or crossed, and that last fillip could very easily be confused with a comma.

Yet it would be so pleasant to be able to lie in bed and listen to the sounds of one's spouse's felt-tip pen and know what she was putting down the very moment it occurred to her. Not long before, on the plane to my sister's wedding, with the infant Bug swaddled and asleep across our laps, I had looked over at Patty, full of contentment at this first trip we were taking since we had become parents, and I had been impressed by the resemblance of her eyelashes to shaving brushes (that same lighter coloration at their ends), but I had hesitated to tell her this—it seemed a poor comparison, demanding a complicated secondary itemization of the features of shaving brushes that were contextually irrelevant—and I felt it was better not to push through the bead curtain of her attention with only it in hand; and then I felt the familiar curiosity about what *was* occupying her attention, and I wanted to ask, "What are you thinking about, Dark Dooley?" But hadn't I been asking her that question much too much lately: dogging her breastfeeding trances with tentative inquiries, because the coincidences or disparities between our thoughts always interested me? It was a form of harassment, or might ultimately become one: it required her to scramble around plucking and arranging recent transients into spoken sequence. A few nights prior to this plane ride I had come across a piece of paper near the phone on which she had written "$30,000" several times, and "Jane JANE JANE Jane." I asked her what it meant, and she said that it wasn't for me to know: that is, she would tell me if it was in any way interesting but really it was totally uninteresting, a doodle she had made while on the phone with her friend, not even worth the time it took to explain why I would be disappointed at its lack of interest. I whined at her to tell me anyway, pounding on the arm of the couch, insisting that everything about her was interesting, that there must be some novel or revealing feature to it, something that would give a finer grain to my knowledge of her, that (as Francis Thompson said in a review of Yeats's early poetry) "Always true is always new." But for the first time, she didn't say, "All right, I'll tell you, but I warned you it's dumb," and instead flatly refused. Another time she had stopped in the middle of a sentence, saying, "Never mind, it's stupid," and here too I had begged her to finish her story, until finally she stopped laughing at my persistence and lost her temper, saying that sometimes she just wanted to protect from public scrutiny a little notion that she had mistakenly let halfway out. These late shieldings of her minor processes of self from me had left traces of uncertainty that now darkened my intention to ask her what was on her mind.

Yet I suspected, because travel so often provoked life-summational emotions (and especially now, with the sensation of the new Bug asleep on our laps), that this would be one of those times when if I did get a peek into her thoughts I would be rewarded by a specific clump of happiness that I would be permanently grateful to have learned; one of those powerful, marriage-

17

reinforcing confidences. So I thought I ought for both our sakes to ask her—but as a concession to her right to privacy I decided to vary the probe by giving my face a slightly craven and servile expression and by using the traditional porch-swing wording, "Penny for your thoughts?" in a uvularly hoisted Pee-wee Herman voice. But Jesus, I thought, a penny! Who came up with this ridiculously cheap valuation? A shilling, a quarter, a kingdom! When I was in fourth grade, my father once offered me a whole dime a page to work my way through a thick elementary Latin textbook (I made forty cents, counting the copyright and title pages); surely the possession of a set of Patty's current thoughts, even if they seemed to her lowly or undistinguished, would be more interesting and precious to me than those unyielding pages of grammar had been. Another time, a few years later, my father and I were driving to my grandparents' place in New Jersey, when he turned down the radio and said, "Hey, so what are you thinking about?" I told him that I had been trying to reconstruct all the transitions between all the subjects (Bach on the radio, the theory of lift, the possibility of infinite-speed gearboxes, new bicycle designs that took better advantage of the thigh muscles, etc.) that we had talked about since we'd driven off at six-thirty that morning; and he said, shaking his finger in "you've got a point there" approval, "That's good, good mental exercise—you should try to do that a lot."

The recollection of my father's deeply flattering advice strengthened my determination: I simply had to intrude on Patty's reflections by asking her what they were. I was on the point of leaning toward her ear when she suddenly turned smiling at me and said, "What strange plans are you hatching, Snakeboy? You have quite a conspiratorial look." So I told her everything I could remember, from the sight of her eyelashes backlit against the airplane window a few seconds before to the rash decision just then to interrupt her inner life. The shaving-brush comparison pleased her more than I expected (her father still used one), and the fact that I had been thinking a nice thing about her may have been enough to click her trust in me up a notch, since she then said that while I had been weighing whether to break the silence, she had been thinking that she didn't care that the position of the hot Bug on her lap was certainly going to leave wrinkles in her dress, and that once, when she was still in college and I was in my first year at Neimtzow Controls, she had put on a green cotton dress to visit me and had stood in the aisle of the uncrowded train all the way from Philadelphia to Boston so that the cotton wouldn't be wrinkled when I met her in the station. She'd never told me this before! A marriage-reinforcer.

Soon after my sister's wedding, Patty began writing every night in the notebook. As hard as I continued to listen, I couldn't make out her meaning; but the sound itself, mixing with my little theories as to which events of that day she might select to put down, had a delicate confidingness of its own that I began to depend on: it was like the sounds that came from the family gerbil in my room as I lay in the dark thinking about whether I should break the news to my best fourth-grade friend Jim Heydemann that I alone of all people in the world had the ability to see individual air molecules as they vibrated about two feet below the ceiling in the dark: crisp sunflower-seed nibblings from the un-seen cage (in the steady polyrhythms of clunky wire-service ma-chines that used to lend urgency and dignity to the instant just before a station break on the evening news); the nice sense of intently focused, glossy-eyeballed activity going on nearby, while I could direct my speculations frictionlessly in any direction, no specific seed or sentence to finish. Or no: I listened even harder to

Patty's writing and realized that I had been misdescribing it to myself. I had been unintentionally falsifying what I heard by imposing on it the knowledge that she was writing strings of words, when in fact, if I mentally disconnected the sound from its source, I would find that the information-rich scribbling produced by word formation was insignificant in comparison to the very high short lisps that took place *between* words and groups of words, as Patty moved the side of her hand a short distance to the right in order to establish a new temporary base for her handwriting. These papery swishes, the "negative spaces" between scribble units, contributed far more to the emotional soothingness of the sound of her diary-keeping than the word noise did—just as, when you listen to someone drawing your likeness, what is nicest are the occasional big hisses you hear as eraser grit is swept from the page. When I was eight and my sister was seven, my mother taught a series of art classes for high school kids at the Memorial Art Gallery, and she tried out many of the lessons on us first. Some, like the "negative spaces" lesson, were taken from Nicolaïdes, while others, like her impossible assignment to "draw the inside of a pillow," were her own invention. Possibly because I had been hit with the romance of negative spaces so early, I had turned against it, and became impatient with art historical discussions in college that drew attention to the painted light between tree trunks as opposed to the real tree trunks themselves, and with the overemphasis in science classes on "paradigm shifts" to the detriment of "normal science"; but it felt good years later to come back around, as you almost always did eventually, to acquiescing to the partial truth of some overhyped observation—and I was pleased to have returned to an appreciation of negative space not by leafing through a book of Klimt's landscapes or by reading about William James's "intention of saying a thing," but by recognizing that it was more truthful to downplay the scribble and focus on the hand-slide in my own wife's record of our life. Probably it was the other way around in the eighteenth century: when the Duke of Gloucester said the famous scribble-scribble-scribble thing to Gibbon, the scratch of quill nibs did indeed rival the sound of one's hand sliding to a new spot below the line—in fact, the sound of a quill pen was probably quite close to the sound of my eyelashes scraping against the pillowcase every time I blinked, thinking about how Patty's writing sounded.

I listened some more; I began to question how her hand knew when to slide. It seemed to shunt over every other word or so. But was the process entirely mechanical, the movement instigated as the wrist reached some threshold of pivoting tension, or was there a higher semivoluntary involvement that influenced the decision, say, to press on until the comma before repositioning—much as one will sometimes squeeze out a last gasping teaspoonful of lung air to finish shouting an angry thought rather than incur the mild loss of contentious momentum that a breath would demand?

4
···· · · · · · 4 · · · · · ···

I BLEW A SLOW, LONGISH PUFF OF AIR in the direction
of the mobile of inspection slips to see whether I could make it
move from where I sat, across the room from the crib, or whether
the impulse would die out along the way. At first, the mobile
didn't move. When Patty and I were engaged and had just rented
an apartment together, three times I heard her in another room
making sighs of happiness—though, like most of the breathy
words that denote emotion sounds ("sob," "pant," "cluck in dis-
approval," etc.), "sigh" is misleadingly over-general, and not a
good match for the deep intake and the semivoiced "Heem!" that
she actually made; and the happiness was possibly overlaid with
some relief, or with the fading presences of bad earlier fall seasons
when we broke up on weird pretexts, or when she told me firmly
that we could never get married because she could never trust me,
because how could I have gone off after she had given me that
wicker picnic basket for Valentine's Day, stocked with blue
enamel plates covered with a white splatter pattern like the inside
of a clothes washer, and with small jars of pickled peppercorns

22

and pickled baby eggplants and pickled Brussels sprouts? How could I have gone off after she had spent five solid minutes observing with wonder the way my proverbials moved up and down ceaselessly like an oil-well pump as I lay otherwise motionless sprawled on the bed? Her sigh meant, "And after all that, here I am in this apartment with a balcony, engaged, having just had a shower and wearing a yellow shirt that I like, with the living room starting to look all right, and what a close call it all was! How easily it all could not have happened! But no, I *knew* that it would happen seven years ago, that time I told Anita in the cafeteria that I had decided I wanted to have sex with him!" She didn't sigh that way anymore, though I thought she still loved me quite a bit and may in fact have been happier than in those first months, but I was pleased to be reminded of that time now: the very beginning of a marriage always takes on an attractively primeval, sedum-like quality in retrospect, no matter how many years the two of you knew each other beforehand. In those first weeks in that apartment, for instance, we didn't have any doorstops, and the cheap hollow-core doors were always being sucked into slamming shut as outside gusts created temporary vacuums in one room or another—so that we suddenly would have privacy imposed on us and could knock on the newly closed door and pay a visit to each other and then leave the door open and feel the windy hugeness of all three rooms of our new life together.

Then one day after work I went to a Woolworth's to buy some candles at Patty's request, and was unable to find any in celadon at the Washington Street store's sadly neglected "Candle Center"— for though celadon had become a lot more popular since she had first pointed it out to me in college, in a Classici dell'Arte book of Pontormo's frescos, it had not yet reached Woolworth's, and on the way to the register I passed another aisle of housewares and caught sight of some dark-red rubber doorstops in bubble packs, and I thought, "Hey, one of the things I can do is have a married life with a woman in an apartment that has doorstops! I can simply buy them!" In the house I grew up in, a mysterious brick, left by the previous owners and covered in floral needlepoint, had served to hold open the inner front door, and because Jim Heydemann and I had played catch with this "Home Sweet Home" brick one day in the driveway, and had dropped it many times, the inaccessible ballast, repeatedly broken, made audible cereal-box noises as one footed it into place. It had never occurred to me that any other doorstop for the front door was possible. And yet I had always envied normal households that had (besides aluminum screen doors whose hissing pistons could be locked into the open position by moving a little ring) doorstops wedged permanently into place under the open swinging kitchen door. I bought five doorstops from Woolworth's that day (extra, so we would never run out, no matter what size of house we ended up with) and jammed them in place, enjoying the simplicity of the concept: as pure a machine as the fulcrum, but charged with the task, not of making displacement easier, but of enforcing stability.

And it was quite characteristic of both of us that the domestic success that pleased Patty most in those first weeks of marriage was assigning a special drawer to hold a number of pairs of candles of sophisticated colors (whose white wicks were always lit for a few seconds before we had someone over for dinner, because it was apparently polite not to cause secret distress in the dinner guest by implying that the hosts had been obliged to junk the old candles and bring out a brand-new set to be melted half away by the end of

the meal, and because the holding of the wick-blackening flame
to each candle marked the loss of virginity of the table setting,
allowing the guest to go ahead and mess up the perfect placement
of the food on his plate without compunction), while the success
that pleased me most, on the other hand, was owning five wedges
of dark-red rubber to shove under the doors.

Patty would have had a name for that dark-red rubber, too: the
red of the air hoses in gas stations and the ones that led to the
diving helmets in *Red Rackham's Treasure*, of toilet plungers, of
the seals under the lids of peanut butter jars before they moved to
a white sprayed-on compound, of the rubber finger-thimbles you
used to flip quickly through sheaves of paper. Brick red? Maybe it
was called brick red. I owed all my knowledge and awareness of
colors to Patty. Indeed, that morning when the Bug was a few
weeks old and I had walked into the kitchen holding the handful
of inspection slips and said what beautiful colors they were, I had
been conscious of a slight sense of *trying out* the idea that the
colors themselves could be the quality of the slips that gave me
pleasure, and not the coloristically drab but procedurally engross-
ing production line of clothes manufacturing they implied; and
aware also of wanting to prove to Patty that I was making progress
in my ability to find things in the world that she would like, and
bring them to her as gifts. Covertly I would study her as she looked
at a shelf full of china gravy boats at an antique store, watching
her eye movements and trying to learn, without having her spell it
out, which gravy boats she rejected and which attracted her and
in what order; and I did the same thing as we flipped through a
glossy house magazine together. Sometimes I would make a stab
at appreciation—"That's a pretty nice wallpaper?"—and then
award myself some grade, like a B minus, after hearing her

25

judicial, "Yes, although I'm not convinced by the swags, and that end table looks forlorn there."

And she too was at work on learning why the things that pleased me did please me, testing her progress against my reactions. This reciprocally crossed effort to master the other's interests meant a temporary subjugation of one's own, so that, for example, when Patty pointed out a beautiful book of photographs and engineering drawings of gears (sepia, gray, black) in a Rizzoli bookstore, not saying, "Hey, here's something *you'll* like, Spank-victim," but rather, "Oh, how beautiful these gears are!" as if an enthusiasm for mechanical engineering had been innate in her, I had to force myself back into my old technologically appreciative self and go, "Oh, Momma! Cycloids! Much better than old Edward's shots of the green pepper!"—when I myself had been intently scanning the same table of books to predict the one (*Blue and White China? Long Island Landscape?*) that she would have exclaimed about had she not been trying to second-guess my exclamation. And thus we both reinforced a more fixed earlier self with its simpler enthusiasms in order to reward each other for having seen and understood them, even while our more fluid present selves began adjusting to new admixtures and we became proud of how far we had left those primitively in-character tastes behind.

Ah, but this now introduced an interesting doubt about Patty and the inspection slips. Up until now, the fact that she had been delighted enough by their pale colors and simple texts to devote two entire Bug-naps to threading them together into something for our daughter, something that *could never be thrown away,* constituted a big confirmatory success for me. She had genuinely liked the colors that I had pulled like Bullwinkle from my brown tweed pocket! I had felt as if Slade had given me an honorary degree. But now I questioned her motives: perhaps she had been only mildly interested in those colors when I held them out to her. In the course of her pregnancy, and in those early days of nursing, her own color sense, she told me, had undergone a lurid upheaval: her old subtle favorites lost their savor, and, for the first time ever, she had experienced deep throbs of mental pleasure simply in staring at a plastic bag of raw cranberries. She brought home the Better Homes and Gardens *Five Seasons Cranberry Book*, and made Chicken Ruby, Fruited Pork Chops, and barbecued Cranberry Whirlibirds (also a chicken dish), as well as cupcakes and Best-ever Cranberry Muffins (all from recipes thoroughly assayed for "family appeal, practicality, and deliciousness" in the Better Homes and Gardens Test Kitchen), not out of physical craving, but just for the satisfaction of manipulating those lacquered spheres of color, boiling them and spooning them; and one weekend we traveled in Ocean Spray's double-decker bus to a bog to watch the floating berries being roped toward a machine that shot them in an arterial gush into a truck. In the midst of this hormone-fed enthusiasm, she must have looked at the wan fan of inspection slips I had waved excitedly, the whispy celadon of LINING PRESS and the Alice blue of ARMHOLE PRESSING, and inwardly thought, "How hopelessly far behind me he is." But after I had left for work and the Bug was drifting to sleep at her breast, maybe her eye again rested on the inspection slips on the table, and maybe she then remembered how excited she had been in her senior year to find an inexpensive lamp at the discount store in Ardmore to furnish her very first apartment, a lamp whose porcelain base was the precise celadon hue of one of the veils in the Pontormo poster she was having shrink-mounted to hang on her wall. I had taken the train down from Boston that time to see her, and attended closely while she pointed to details of the same Pontormo in her Classici dell'Arte book and demonstrated how they matched the lamp; and then she brought out a dry, soap-stiff washcloth (mine, in fact: she never used washcloths in the shower, another sexually exciting fact about her) to show that because of the paling effect of the soap it too exactly matched the lamp and the Pontormo veil. It wouldn't be right to say that I was unimpressed: I immediately liked the ponderously dinosaural *-on* termination mapped over such a circumspect color, and I was pleased to be linked to someone like Patty who knew about it, but though I crowed politely, I couldn't see any special merit to the tint itself—and almost certainly she sensed this failing. I had never heard of Pontormo, and the only discussion of color in my one semester of art history that had held my attention had been the textbook's blowup of the spectral waterdrops on the backs of Delacroix's swimmers in hell: optical pedagogy, not pure color itself, was what had gotten to me then.

As it happened, later that afternoon I caught the cord of the new lamp with my foot so that it lurched onto the radiator and was multiply chipped. Embarrassed by my clumsiness, I was crabby rather than apologetic; I said that she'd *said* it was a cheap lamp, and we could certainly get another the next day; and she said that it was the last one of that color in the store and that it had been her first purchase for her first apartment and all she wanted from me was a simple "I'm very sorry I hurt your lamp" and not dismissive references to its price; and so I said I was sorry and bought some glue and spent an absorbing fifteen minutes reuniting the three chips with the base: in concentrating on fitting those pieces together, delighted by the gritty ease with which they found their settings, their crack lines disappearing even more completely than the seams between stacked checkers or between the wing-pieces on model airplanes, I filled my visual sense with that color and began to understand it. As she once told me years later, to comfort me as she glued together a Pier 1 Chinese serving dish of hers that I had broken by too carelessly mounding pans in the drainer (that time I was apologetic!): in repairing the object you really ended up loving it more, because you now knew its eagerness to be reassembled, and in running a fingertip over its surface you alone could feel its many cracks—a bond stronger than mere possession.

But even after staring for fifteen minutes at the lamp base, beginning to sense the crudity of my previous poster-paint idea of green, I struggled against the incipient refinement. That afternoon, Patty came back with some new towels in a washed-out pink color. She put them on the towel rack and held the celadon washcloth to them, and asked me to come look. Didn't the colors together against the white tiles remind me of the time we visited Anita in Los Angeles and stayed for two nights in that little motel with a balcony? The clean feeling of the colors together—the sense of sunlit balcony stucco and cloudless blue sky? I said it did. She came over and kissed me on the neck noisily, and I added: "Ah—you know, the pink of the hickey you are giving me plus the pale gray of my T-shirt remind me of that pleasant half hour with you in Bombay, when the junks drifted against the cool walls of the Jewish quarter and the Kaboulis limped in the lengthening shadows of the Hakalinki trees."

Patty laughed very slightly ("hickey" was stupid: we never gave each other *hickeys*) and said, "We better get ready if we want to be there by seven." She stood for a moment before her tiny, packed closet. The lighter clothes were narrow bands of color randomly distributed in the woollier press of darker skirts and coats, forming a pattern like a spectrograph. She took hold of the sleeve of a striped shirt, pulled it free, and held it here and there, against a number of dark masses, shaking her head. Then she let go of the sleeve. I knew she was very near crying. I followed her around, saying, "What is it? What is it?" and she said, "Nothing, never mind, nothing," not looking at me.

Finally I said, "Is it about the towels?" and she nodded.

I began a string of sorry-okays.

"It's not," she explained, "that you insulted me or hurt my feelings. Maybe it is! But it's more that I wanted so much to be able to say how the colors together reminded me of the motel, and all I did was sound hollow and pretentious."

"No! You didn't sound hollow and pretentious! I loved the towels in conjunction with the washcloth!"

"You were right to mock me."

"I was just being playful! Really and honestly I was moved by the link between these towels and the Pontormo and the lamp and that weekend in the motel with the balcony. The combination held the same feeling! My limping Kaboulis were just trying to compete with your nicer, truer memory!"

"All right. Let me take my shower."

So six years later, when she saw the celadon inspection slip on the kitchen table at the height of her maternal cranberry phase, it may have pleased her only secondarily, as a reference to her past and as evidence of my limited progress. By then possibly celadon had been the tablecloth color of choice in too many hotel renovations and magazine makeovers; constructing the mobile was merely her way of helping me to fuse my still tentative, anxious colorimetry into my permanent, careless, inborn inclination for things with moving parts. The motivating proportions had probably been:

50%   a wish to make something nice for the Bug to look up at in her crib
35%   fondness for my continued apprenticeship in taste
15%   genuine pleasure in the colors

For a second the fifteen-percent figure made me unhappy, and then I thought, Fine, yes, I *welcome* all this imperfect mingling—I want this circling refluxion of our old reconditioned pleasures and our new genuine ones to continue for years, decades, until it becomes impossible to trace backward the history of any particular liking, just as it was impossible to unstir the rash dollops of red or yellow tint my mother used to add to the custom-mixed paints she got from Sears: she used old peanut butter jars as receptacles, and sat cross-legged in the side yard pouring imperceptibly different yellow-greens from one jar to another, refining the color that she wanted for the porcelain-knobbed dresser in my sister's room, though the young technician in the paint department at Sears had with apparently scientific precision injected what seemed to me a perfectly acceptable series of squirts of yellow, cyan, and magenta from the paint organ into a white base, according to the recipe in a notebook for the sample chip my mother had matched to the border of a cloth calendar. She was closing in now on her idea; she had long since made use of the one free stirrer that came with the can of paint, and was now "warming" the dresser-color-to-be by dipping a pencil in a tiny can of old Rust-Oleum and holding it above the peanut butter jar so that a stream of red fell, disappearing entirely at first and pooling in an invisible bulb of unmixedness at the heart of the host hue, and then later, as the pencil's burden lightened, thinning to a stretched rubber band's breadth frail enough to remain caught on the surface, recording in Spirograph patterns the minute trembles of her hand and the light breezes that unplumbed the paint's angle of descent. Again she dipped the pencil in the red and held it over the jar; and then, although I was sure that she could have had no real knowledge of how large the reservoir of potential warmth was that hung somewhere in the midst of the yellow-green, waiting to tint it, she said, "I think that will do it," and stirred, and then she poured this new mixture into another jar of slightly lighter color, thereby interpolating a shade between them—and that was the color my sister's small dresser was painted, a color that may have been close to celadon but was probably more of an ocher, that formed the background to the brown rubber bands I stretched between the porcelain knobs in L shapes and triangles, imagining I was threading tan magnetic tape around the capstans of a tape recorder, from which I plucked unpleasant tunes with my eyes closed. These painting projects of my mother's were one of the reasons why there were whole months during summers of house-fixup that we had no pencils around to take phone messages or leave notes to each other that tomorrow was garbage day, although at other times, when my mother was teaching after-school art classes, we had a sudden influx of nearly acceptable implements: Grumbacher HHs that left a faint trace on the page, and red grease pencils that were unrolled rather than sharpened, Wolff's charcoal pencils, and bars of pure graphite. My mother had gone to Parsons for two years and afterward, until she became pregnant with me, had worked as a colorist for Greff Fabrics, assigned patterns in outline to fill in as she wished; and possibly as a result of this overexposure to the infinitude of the color chart she almost never mentioned individual tints by name. So Patty was telling me something entirely new by teaching me "celadon"; yet from my mother I already understood that women were the only route out of the brown world: women transformed the wood-paneled male principle, the terrene unctuosity of peanut butter, into the female emanation of World's Fair White breast milk, into dozens of intermediate colors of paint, and, in Patty's later case, as she fed steadily on those dull spoonfuls of Skippy at the outset of her pregnancy, into the subtle gradients of flushes and blue shadows of my own daughter's face.

5

SHE WAS GOING TO SLEEP too quickly, before she had finished enough of the bottle, so I blew gently on her forehead. I had given her a bath that morning: her clean fine bang hair shifted. Her eyes, which had been half shut, opened fully and she saw me again. "Evaporated milk!" I whispered. "Delicious evaporated milk!" I was risking wasting all those moaned stanzas of "Over Hill, Over Dale" by introducing my voice into her doze curve, but I needed a last instant of alertness from her, an acknowledgment by eye contact before she went more completely to sleep that I was the kindly person who held her with her knees slightly bent the way she liked, and who made my sweater fully available to her hand, and who, today, had gotten the rocker to bump with unusual indolence: the proud sponsor of her nap. Her eyelids fell to half again, and her hand resumed its roaming. Her bottle was still about two-thirds full. She had a regular rhythm going: she took three pulls on the nipple and then swallowed, and every other time she swallowed, she made a lovely voiced sigh or hum of exhalation, not unlike Patty's sounds in the first weeks of our engagement—for miraculously, while she drew the milk into her mouth until it formed a large enough pool to trigger a swallow, she was at the same time engaged in breathing through her nose. (Two separate vacuums—a lung vacuum for inhaling, and a mouth vacuum for sucking, were in effect *simultaneously!* She was a remarkable, remarkable daughter.) "It's certainly not going to be a small nose!" said Patty's father when the Bug was only a month old, since Patty's and my noses were both substantial, though in different ways. He made the pronouncement with the same intelligent ironic tone he had used (so Patty related it) two years earlier, when he first saw the somewhat ornate Victorian engagement ring that my widowed maternal grandmother had given me to give to her, and he had said, "Well!—it's certainly not vulgarly discreet." But the Bug's nose, its infantile tininess combining with its monstrous promise, was at the moment one of her nicest features, and the best thing about it was what it shared with all babies' noses: not the gargoylian turn of its wings, which was from Patty's parents, nor the palpable bump at the bridge, which might at puberty bulk itself into a "Beal Breakfront," as those who had married into my mother's family, the Beals, had called it among themselves for several generations—no, what was finest about the Bug's nose was the same amazing thing I had noticed at age five when shown a neighbor's newborn: *it was so clean inside.* You looked into the translucent orange regions and saw surfaces of inconceivable perfection. Any fleck that was visible only pointed up the general pristineness. I loved Patty's nose, of course, though she had been embarrassed by it even into college, when I first met her, and had avoided the very word, using instead, as she flipped through a fashion magazine and evaluated the models' beauty with her roommate Anita, the helpfully indirect phrase "big features," tapping approvingly on faces with noses similar to hers.

Later, when she was braver and confided more in me, she would talk about how some photograph of her made her seem woefully "all nose"—the reason being that she often averted her face just as a snapshot was snapped, so that only her hair and nose and a smiling curve of cheek were captured. Her marginal drawings during class were all of elegant men and women in profile exhibiting variations on her nose—and indeed, the first person she got a crush on in college, though I flirted on the sidelines, was a good-looking Armenian physical-chemistry major with a powerfully bifurcated frontispiece like a late Nixon caricature. I was familiar with the pleasure of nose art myself, but my technique had frozen in sixth grade into a G-shaped eyebrow-nose-nostril unit; I admired Don Martin's noses in *Mad*, and Sprod's, from *Punch*, whose cartoon of a cocktail party full of people with nasal oddities, one of whom was trying to make small talk with a caged parrot, had exerted a strong spell over me ever since 1963, when I was six and we moved into a house whose previous owners had left an anthology, *Best Cartoons from Punch*, along with a hot-water bottle, in a cabinet in the bathroom. Patty's nose was a perfect weight, I thought: something you would want to carry around in your pocket for good luck, like a Roman coin—and in fact sometimes she described its shape as "Roman." As her endearments became bolder and more hermetic after we got married, departing from courtship's Mike, Micky, Mickanore, Norker, Yamanicky, Yaminore, Immiyam, Noser's Yam, Mokey, Inky, Inker, Sphincter, Sphinx, Immanore, Immydear, Sippydear, Simpy sequence—a fluid achievement of Patty's whose evolution I wanted to subject to some sort of microphilological equivalent of Grimm's law of the permutation of Teutonic consonants (*have* Bichakjian et al. taken a hard look at the paedomorphosis of pet names?)—and moving into linguistically inexplicable forms like

Hornefleur, Fatboy, Lowbrow, and Dark Shitter, I became corre-
spondingly audacious and asked her straight out if I could *live in
her nose*. (By the time she was calling me Horn F., we were already
several months into the rival declension of *Bug*: Big Bug, Biggy
Bug, Biggity Bug, Buggy Doo, Biggy Doo, Biggy Dooley, Biggity
Big Bug, Bogo, Biggo, Bugadooley, Boger, Bobey, Little Bober,
Bolo, etc.) Perhaps I was influenced by memories of the coziness
of Bag-End in *The Hobbit* and of Peter Rabbit's firelit bungalow,
and by the cover of *Revolver*, where a miniature Beatle tries to
climb out of Paul's ear canal. When I began to develop crank
theories that many of my Quaker forebears were assimilated
Jews—theories that Patty thought presumptuous and shushed
with a warning "Crinkler!" whenever something made me bring
them up, I began to treasure the shape of both of our noses as
evidence that we each still remained somewhat Jewish; the
Gaudí-like outcomes were attributable to an imperfect consor-
tium between the stereotypically Jewish profile and debasingly
trollish architraves of cartilage, in my case of English Protestant
origin, in hers of Irish Catholic—though even on the Protestant
side I sensed or hoped for a dimmer Jewishness in me further
back. "You wish," said Patty. "You're as pure a Wasp as you could
possibly be." When I started to question who the Puritans had
been anyway but well-to-do dissenting Jews, citing, irrelevantly,
John Jay Chapman, half Jewish himself, on the resemblance of
Puritan portraiture to the likenesses of great Venetian merchants
in the Doge's Palace, I could feel her getting angry and question-
ing inwardly why she was putting up with me—so I stopped. But
I secretly rejoiced that the Bug blended features from both of our
noses, since in that way she might be reassembled into what I
hoped was a more complicatedly Jewish person than either of us
was individually.

Aside from this somewhat abstract genealogical interest I took in the Bug's nose, I took a physical interest as well. When she was only three weeks old and breathing entirely through it, using her mouth only when crying, I would sometimes use two fingertips to block her nostrils. She would try for an instant to continue to inhale, and then, delighted by the light stoppage, she would open her mouth for air with a popping sound and smile. "Hey, hey, hey!" Patty would say mildly. "Don't do that to her."

"She likes it," I would say, but I didn't do it very often. After I had cut down my time at work to two days a week and had really bonded with the Bug, I grew bold one afternoon, stunned at the perfect love-inspiring beauty of her round glowing face as she lay on the changing table studying a small superball she held in her hands, after I had wiped her captivating little coffee bean of a pudendum and put on a new diaper, the air filled with the fresh sound of crinkly plastic as she kicked experimentally, and after I had rolled up the old gel-puffed diaper into a tight hoagie and secured it with its own adhesive tabs: I bent low toward her face, filling her vision with a pretend-amazed expression, and deliberately tasted, or rather touched my tongue tip to the perimeter of, one of her nostril openings. She pushed me away uninterestedly, staring in complete concentration at the swirling blue and red injections in the amber-colored superball (originally a stocking-stuffer from me to Patty, but like many of the toys we had once given to each other, now finding a secondary life as a Bug-diversion), but for me the sensation marked a new stage of love for her, as when a cat touches your hand with its nose and jumps back at the static and yet is willing to try to sniff you again, or when one time in college Patty got out of my dorm bed with only a dark blue T-shirt on and discovered a dime stuck to her bottom, because we had been sleeping all night in change that had poured at some stage of arousal from my pants pockets the night before, and said sleepily, without puzzlement, "Dime on my bottom," and put it on my desk, and I had used it as a bookmark for several years after that, erasing a stripe in it to single it out. The Bug's nostril had the innocent perfection of a Cheerio (and Cheerios were on my mind, since lately we had begun to offer them to her), a tiny dry clean salty ring, so small, with the odd but functional smallness of the tires on passenger planes, or of the smooth rim around the pistil of the brass pump head that you fitted over a tire's stem valve to inflate it to a pressure you preset with a crank on the air machine: at first, as the pump head and the stem valve failed to couple, there was a sharp, wasteful hissing, and the dinger tolled freely, but then you got the surfaces to seal and the air began to flow throatily in—each slow decelerating ding now made the tire change shape slightly, as if it were swallowing, and the sound of the hiss was released *into* the tire, where the extra atmospheres gave it an unusual pent resonance (this was truer of car tires than bicycle tires), like the sounds strong dogs made as they strained at leashes, and familiar also from the transformation of the initial chesty sigh of balloon inflation into a space-age-upward-warping effect as the balloon's limit was reached, or the faint, high, sonar-like suffix of sound that the expensive kind of textured red rubber playground balls added to the prosaic bounce of external impact on concrete: inside, the shock waves flew around the ball (and the balloon and the tire) in unusually high-velocity polyhedrons, delighted by the readiness of their compressed medium to hurry their rebounds and lengthen their term of reverberation. Air, that unparceled and seemingly infinite plenitude, available world-wide, was focused and linearized by the air pump and brought to bear on a single task—and so it was with my lovely Bug, who was able to inhale its transparent liters through a pair of miraculous one-sixteenth-inch portals and as a consequence to live and even to derive amusement from a superball with a swirl in it. "Wild air, world-mothering air," Hopkins called it; air that

> riddles, and is rife
> In every least thing's life

My supreme Bug! My least thing's life! Sometimes when Patty and I were admiring her I would hold my fingers together in an almond shape and put them over the top of the Bug's now blonder head and say, "I knew you when you were *this big*": for that shape of black prenatal hair, outlined by Patty's widening vagine (she dropped the terminal *a* in speaking of it, improving an imperfect word), was my first sight of my daughter, and when fifteen minutes later her blue head dropped into the room, looking as if she had just then closed her eyes in resigned exasperation, like a weary, middle-aged commuter caught in a sudden downpour, the first thing they did was to aspirate her nostrils and mouth with a simple but specialized device, a turquoise squeezable rubber claxon horn, so that she could breathe. As the very first manufac- tured item she had experienced, this nose vacuumer was of considerable sentimental value, but even so I was quite surprised when they gave it to us to take home: what a bonus! It was like the boy I read about not long afterward in the *Weekly World News*. He swallowed a tadpole on a dare with some friends, and several months later complained of stomach pains, and when the doctor snaked a catheter down him and put his eye to the viewfinder to peer into the boy's stomach he jumped in horror, for he saw an eye blinking back at him: the tadpole had grown into a four-pound toad, repudiating all attempts at digestion. And when the toad was safely removed, by a sort of C-section, the doctor gave it to the boy to take home as a pet: a bonus! This image, in turn, of a frog that had matured within a boy's digestive system, took its place in my memory as the inversion of a picture I had often looked up as a boy in one of the early Time-Life books—perhaps one on genetics or evolution: it was of a frog that had been cloned from idioplasm sucked out of a single intestinal cell of another frog. The two frogs were posed side by side, and the artificial sibling was unquestionably complete and froglike in every detail; but I noticed that it wasn't an exact replica: it had a disturbing and somehow gastrointestinal pallor in its mottling, and an unhealthy, pear-shaped, I-was-raised-in-a-petri-dish-and-know-little-of-mud-and-reeds type of body that betrayed its origins. The artificial frog permanently influenced my theory of knowledge: I certainly believed, rocking my daughter on this Wednesday afternoon, that with a little concentration one's whole life could be reconstructed from any single twenty-minute period randomly or almost randomly selected; that is, that there was enough content in that single confined sequence of thoughts and events and the setting that gave rise to them to make connections that would proliferate backward until potentially every item of auto-biographical interest—every pet theory, minor observation, significant moment of shame or happiness—could be at least glancingly covered; but you had to expect that a version of your past arrived at this way would exhibit, like the unhealthily pale frog, certain telltale differences of emphasis from the past you would recount if you proceeded serially, beginning with "I was born on January 5, 1957," and letting each moment give birth naturally to the next. The particular cell you started from colored your entire re-creation.

6

W HO COULD HAVE PREDICTED that the turquoise rubber aspirator she brought home from the hospital, the landmark device that made official her amphibious passage from a liquid life to a gaseous one in the first few seconds after her head emerged, even before the rest of her had gushed out, would quickly become one of her favorite toys—that she would love to squeeze it so that air whooshed in her face? Who could have predicted, after all those months of warm soaking, that bracing puffs of air in general would make her so happy? When the wind gusted up Wollaston Hill and caught her just as we were lifting her from the warmth of her car seat, she would inhalingly make "Fip! Fip!" sounds, squinting flutteringly against the air's surprise, kicking and looking at us in delight for an explanation. "Windy!" I would say. And on the flight to my sister's wedding, the Bug gestured upward toward the personal ventilation jets above our seats, already as captivated by this trio of motorized nostrils as I had been on BOAC trips to Bermuda when I was five, where my grandmother served us stewed prunes with undiluted evaporated

milk for breakfast, and my grandfather once recited "The History
of Doctor Wango Tango" to me on the beach, saying that it had to
be unique to the English edition of *Struwwelpeter*, because it was
too fine a poem to be a translation from the German, and where I
spent hours in the early morning trying to dislodge the chitons
that held the rocks at the end of the beach with a primitive,
Lower-Ordovician vacuum stronger than anything I had encoun-
tered in pulling a suction dart off my forehead or a suction-
mounted pencil sharpener off a Formica table at school. I held her
up so that she could feel the air streaming from the airplane
ventilators, and I showed her how they pivoted in their plastic
sockets, and how they could be screwed one way or another to
vary their amplitude. She made the inhaling seagull cry that at
that period signified sudden joy. Our actual vibrating rush down
the runway and our lift into flight and the clunk of the withdrawn
landing gear did not distract her from her rapt appreciation of the
interior invention: a participatory jet engine for each passenger,
with a cream-colored pointed cone of plastic in its center similar
to the metallic cones at the rear of the impossibly heavy GE
engines outside, whose turbines ground slowly in and out of
phase. It was a calming bit of self-paced instruction in the behav-
ior of compressible fluids; it was even a useful deception of sorts,
since after an hour of feeling that spotlight of air playing over your
face, your thoughts full of the remembered sight of contrails in a
blue sky as seen from earth—the way they first appear like narrow
staves of music a little way behind a very high plane, and gradually fatten into shaving-cream crudities before fading—or of cold
rides in the back of pickup trucks, when your cheek nerves grew
deadened to the insistent flapping of a lock of hair that now
doesn't exist, or of the print ad for Maxell tape in which a man sits
in an armchair and experiences a blast of *La Mer* from his

speakers that sinks him deep into the cushions and flings his tie over his shoulder and tips the shade of the standing lamp, you began to think that if the real jet engines were to fail, the plane would float to earth on the output of these tame little verniers alone, as in the parlor trick in which ten guests each use one finger to lift a heavy volunteer—and as the plane lost altitude and the captain flipped desperately through the technical manuals muttering, "It's *got* to be a bad chip!" one alert hero would jump up and say, "Turn your air vents to full, people!" and Ernest Borgnine would passionately chime in, "The man's right! Do as he says!" and every arm would extend, so that from the smoking section you had the impression of an elephant herd reaching their prehensile noses for leafy leftovers on higher branches, and the plane's descent would slow to a pilotable rate, and as we drifted lower and lower over the water, like the brave Frenchmen who crouched in the wicker passenger basket of the damaged and half-empty balloon as it ladled through enormous wavetops in a terrifying illustration for *Mysterious Island* (the nineteenth-century use of wicker is part of what gives ballooning such a Fragonardian, picnicky feel), or like the later Frenchmen who belly-landed on the beach in *Tintin and the Red Sea Sharks*, when we finally slapped down onto the ocean, nobody would be dead: saved yet again by cooperative action and by our own cabin pressure system.

These air nozzles were in fact one of a number of details you could control or adjust from your seat that offered you the illusion that you were actually in charge of the aircraft: the tray tables were landing gear to be stowed and unstowed, the Phillips head screws were buttons that activated various wing lights and radar antennae, the forbidden stewardess-call button released a very big bomb, the tilt-adjustment button kicked in powerful afterburners that threw you backward in your seat, the opaque portshades that slid down from inside the wall of the plane (like the either-or eyelids of one of my sister's dolls that descended with unrealistic slowness because of a cantilevered weight inside the doll's head which I discovered by cutting through the molded contours of its rubber hair) were heat shields that you deployed as the craft plunged directly into the rice-grain ferment of the sun; and when you were safely through the center of the solar system, and you coolly flipped up the top on the armrest ashtray, an airfoil flap would unsheath itself out on the patchwork wing, where there were even more beautiful mid-tone varieties of gray than in the nail and screw bins in smaller hardware stores, a platinum-process print of the fields below, and where each rivet had a shadow from years in the airstream; and the pitch of your banked, rib-crushing turn toward home would be at exactly the angle at which you had set the ashtray's lid.

Only much later did I begin to realize that all that childish poking and seat adjustment had been irritating to the strangers in front of and behind me: that (at least on short flights) we were not really meant ever to push the seat to its extreme restful tilt, and that in tilting it way back solely for the purpose of taking possession of a window that had been only halfway in our seat area (the seats and the windows were puzzlingly out of synchronization), we were being rude to the woman behind us, and especially that any rough treatment of our tray-table latches during flight simulation exercises was transmitted straight through seat foam to the back of the person ahead. We were taught the Golden Rule in first and second grades, but it was only after I had begun reviewing TV commercials for a new arts magazine and was flying back from a stormy punctuational session with a copy editor there—a time when I thought I had lost all sensitivity to the physical interiors of airplanes and wanted, instead of thinking about the design of air nozzles, to continue reading Pattison's life of Isaac Casaubon—that I noticed and was first bothered by a rough stowage of the tray table behind me (by an adult!), and even then I initially thought not with irritation but with surprise and interest that my absorption in a piece of learned intellectual biography could be interrupted simply by some dufe closing a latch at my back, and I went on to wonder whether in twenty years, when Boeing was begging for loan guarantees and sleek airships by Daewoo and Honda with perfect safety records were taxied on every runway, the humble latches on the tray table would be one of the first things in the new non-U.S. planes to announce their instant superiority, despite the fact that once our tray tables had exemplified the state-of-the-art Murphy-bed modernism of a design sense energized by the war; and I felt pity and shame for American plane engineers who had failed to see that thirty years of improvements in the on/off switch, the suitcase closure, the cassette ejection system, the umbrella lock, the calculator button—refinements almost entirely of Asian origin, without which we would still be lost in a stamped-steel twilight of toggle switches, too powerful springs, and rough metal-to-metal frictive contact—that all these parallel novelties were demanding that we dig deeper and find some subtler sort of click or even a clickless but convincing thumplet, like the final leg of the closing of a mason jar, that would remain undetectable even by a sleeping princess in the seat ahead. And later in that same plane ride, instead of feeling hate for this man behind me who in his late forties had not yet learned to stow his tray table without interrupting the reading of a fellow passenger, this man who was too coarse apparently ever to have been bothered by a rough stowage behind *him*, though he looked to have logged tens of thousands of flight miles a year, I simply used extreme care in closing my own table after dinner: I painstakingly clutched the top of the seat ahead of me and, thus stably based, used that thumb to squeeze the table under the fastener before I allowed it to slide into place, imagining as I did so that I was closing the coffin on the U.S. tradition of industrial design.

And yet, if the Japanese designers did get rid of personal air outlets, murmuring contemptuously among themselves about "barbaric holdovers from the infancy of cabin pressurization," I expected to feel, the first time I noticed their absence, the same sort of long-awaited jolt of grief I felt when in the early seventies, intent on being a composer, I came across horrifying articles in the Arts and Leisure section with titles like "Is the Symphony Orchestra Dead?" Like a reporter assigned the obituary page, I gathered my envoical emotions together ahead of time to be ready for the loss: I recalled how I once tried to stretch a balloon around an air nozzle but was ordered to sit down before I found out whether it would inflate; and how, while my sister was occupied with a connect-the-dot book, I very stealthily stole her air and aimed it so that I could revel in a twin convergence; and how, pretending to study the stewardess-call button, I pointed my mother's, my sister's, and my own nozzles toward my sister and turned them all on full, so that the corner of her half-connected rabbit page flapped out of control. As soon as I was sure she was going to cry, I returned nonchalantly to *The Family of Man*, feigning interest in the shots of dust bowls and calloused hands, but in fact fixing in my mind the straining images of the childbirth sequence—the incredible full-lipped ugly powerful arousing frown of the woman pushing amid the hospital sheets—for it, along with a pen-and-ink drawing in a Dover book of Heinrich Kley's drawings, showing a tribal woman giving suck to a foot-

and-a-half-tall baby elephant at each full breast, their squeezed mammalian yieldingness beautifully captured by repeatingly sinuous pen strokes, was my pornography between the ages of seven and nine. But despite hundreds of examples of calculated meanness to my sister, on airplanes, on car rides, at dinner tables, she still loved me enough to invite me to her wedding; indeed, she wanted me to be one of the people who read a little biblical something at the ceremony; and it was only on the way to this wedding, holding my Bug, the product of my own marriage, up to the air vent above us and seeing how entranced she was by it, that my appreciation of it and the screws and the footrest and the tufted-cloud design on the wall that separated us from first-class passengers, and the portshades and the ashtrays, all returned; and I wondered for the first time whether the shape of the nozzle's inner cone was in fact more than decorative, whether it functioned aerodynamically to focus the outflow into a coherent column and allowed it to continue, even at the hissiest stage near shutoff, to offer a palpable incumbency of coolness—unlike the gun-sprayers on garden hoses, which just before the flow of water was completely cut off created instead a Panamanian circular fan of mist on a plane perpendicular to the direction you were pointing the hose, so that you couldn't mist the delicate poppy three feet in front of you unless you aimed away from it and misted yourself as well, or else strengthened your grip on the sprayer's handle so that the flow became injuriously direct. In the hectic last months of design, had the same engineer who had just finished putting the final touches on the turbine's taper been hired away from GE and assigned the cabin details, and had he miniaturized the same principle, smiling to himself?

Participating in my sister's wedding made my own marriage more fixed and comprehensible; I had to be jostled from behind before I took care with the tray table myself; I had to see my Bug love the air nozzle before my own curiosity about it revived. And in holding the Bug up until my arms trembled, I thought I felt the force of some wider, more emotional golden rule that stated that only after having experienced something from both sides— breaking up with someone and being yourself broken up with, and even being born and later assisting at a birth were other examples—did you stand any chance of understanding the event fully. But then, immediately afterward, I was embarrassed, be- cause I realized that this "both sides" idea, which I thought was the outcome of an upsurge of personal feeling at traveling to my sister's wedding and showing the Bug the air vent, was due mainly to the Joni Mitchell song about clouds and dual perspectives that I must have heard (since I now discovered that I had been hum- ming it to myself for over an hour) on the airport Muzak while we were waiting to board.

7

I WAS SURPRISED to catch sight of some unusual movement in the Bug's mobile. LINING PRESS was wagging perceptibly on its thread, wanting to turn, and the whole assembly seemed for a moment inclined to revolve clockwise. Then it grew still. At first I attributed the motion to a draft from a window, but the shades, even the shade-pulls, showed nothing. Could I have had something to do with it? Could the strong experimental puff I had directed across the room some *twenty seconds earlier* have only just then arrived? I thought of the warm, lip-focused airstream surging forward a few feet and then quickly losing itself in increasingly minor efforts at displacement. My diaphragm wasn't nearly in the shape it had been when for three days I had crammed for my own tenth-birthday party by trying repeatedly to blow out an entire lit candelabrum, amazed that people approached this nakedly public moment of wish-making and potential humiliation after going a whole *year* without practice; or when later I was a French horn major at the Eastman School of Music and I could blow up balloons without getting pop-eyed with strain; and my postmusical lip, too, probably couldn't now hold the necessarily narrow aperture to aim and concentrate the air well enough to force it through so much space. Yet perhaps in dying out, my puff had set in motion, or reinforced, larger, slower roomwide currents that had eventually reached the region of the crib. Or maybe that first puff would never have reached the mobile if I hadn't a moment later blown the second small breath onto the Bug's forehead, where it had spread, enveloping her hair and then falling away gradually floorward, like Tennyson's rarefied high-altitude waterfalls, which

> . . . spill
> Their thousand wreaths of dangling water-smoke,
> That like a broken purpose waste in air

—and then, in reaching the floor, unbroken, unwasted, hooked into some sort of low-level system of excitation eddies in the boundary layer that hurried it over the dhurrie rug and at the fringe lifted itself up again where the air was warmer near the windows to brush the inspection slips from underneath, at the very same moment that the last feeble fingers from my directly aimed but slower-moving first breath were signaling their invisible visitation as well. Recently I had been reading some of Marie Boas Hall's scholarly account of Robert Boyle's experiments with the air pump, and I kept encountering citations from one of Boyle's books, the posthumous *General History of the Air.* And on my locker at Eastman, where I kept my horn when I was in orchestration and theory classes, I once taped (with typical freshman self-importance) something I had come across in Lockspeiser's biography of Debussy—unfortunately phrased but bracing nonetheless: "Listen to no one," it quoted Debussy as saying, "unless to the passing wind which tells us the history of the world." Boyle's magnificent title had reminded me of Debussy's firm precept—which, unfortunately, I had completely failed to apply as a music student, spending whole days in fact in the listening room of Eastman's Sibley Music Library with a pair of heavy, greasy headphones on, following the score of *La Mer* and unsuccessfully trying to master its technical secrets, only partially convinced, as the miniature score's thousands of unenlightening notes flew by, by my own theory that the abruptly chopped-off crescendi that Debussy used to create his fantastic open-boat effects of crested loomings and tossings collapsing cyclically into earlier states and then rising up again could be explained by his several early trips to Russia, where the tape-played-backward sounds that to the Western ear are characteristic of Russian speech might have inspired him to use the orchestra to simulate inhalational inversions of those traditional phrasal envelopes which build toward or retreat from a cymbal-assisted climax, effects that Stravinsky, though a native speaker, merely appropriated in the chopped gong-rolls near the end of the *Rite*— while around me, sitting at other carrels, clamped within other greasy headphones, a music history student cramming for finals nodded off, numbed by too much Palestrina, and a pianist with Serkin in his ears mimed a tricky run on the woodgrain, rising transcendentally up at an angle on one clenched buttock muscle, and a music education student triangulated the Sibelius symphony assigned for introductory conducting class with brutal housepainting flips of her pencil. Lately, as Boyle's *General History of the Air* title, along with his quaint vocabulary ("exsuction," "elastical particles," "associated effluviums of a multitude of corpuscles of very differing natures"), and Debussy's notion of a history of the world told in wind, consorted in the near vestibules of my attention, I had begun to feel *primed for awe*: and now, this afternoon, my aerial awe softly arrived. My daughter and I were bathed in a roomful of vortical unfurlings that moved within and past each other as slowly as a tai chi devotee practicing his transitions from pose to pose at dawn in an unsafe park. This room was astir—astir with history. If, using some as yet undeveloped high-resolution technique of flow visualization, I filmed the motion of a cubic yard of air around the mobile of inspection slips for twenty minutes, and if I studied that film for four hours a day, during the Bug's two naps—just looked at it, leaned into the idea of it with my entire self—at various speeds, and took the videotape from one international congress on turbulence to another, and made men of science look at it so that I could read in their polite expressions some of the particular complexities it offered their more geometrically manipulative minds, would I begin to feel that I could deduce from its veils of infinitesimal insurgence and reversion the objects in the room around which the air had flowed before it entered this domain of record? Would I deduce the shapes of the half-inflated plastic globe and the cheese grater on the rug, the superball in the fireplace, my dusty collection of mechanical coin-sorters on one of the bookshelves—and infer that a man breathing steadily through his nose in a rocking chair rocking at roughly one cycle every two seconds had held a baby also breathing through her nose on the verge of sleep? Assuming a fixed set of room dimensions, would I come up with seven, or sixty-one, or thousands, of dramatically different object placements and dual puff sources (or, since we each had two nostrils, quadratic puff sources) that could have made the air move in just that way—or only one? And if I kept looking, could I detect and read the vestigial pulsations inflicted on this yard of air by the movements of Patty's pen the night before as she described yesterday's Bug-delights in her notebook, or those of Gibbon's agitating feather as he scribbled the closing words of his history of the world two hundred years before? No? Not possible? Would I die without knowing the true history of the air, not world-wind-wide, but even confined to twenty minutes in a small cubic area of my daughter's room? I wanted to roar something defiant against this stifling limit to understanding: and I remembered the calming sensation of roaring at full volume directly into a pillow and feeling your outburst sift slowly into the antique atmosphere between the down's barbules, which had felt no humid influx since the last time you wept profoundly enough to infiltrate that preserve of old emotion, or laughed to the limit of breath into it as your father played the opening of Bach's D-minor Fantasy on your back to tickle you, at your request. How could my mother *ever* have expected us to "draw the inside of a pillow"? Nothing in *Mr. Tompkins Inside Himself,* or Mandelbrot, or the lung sequence in *Fantastic Voyage,* or Martin Gardner's topological columns, could have prepared my sister and me for the impossible mental involution of attempting to imagine one's pencil investigating the poorly lit interior surfaces of one's own pillow, that reliquary of sneezes and nosebleeds, while remaining in contact with the fixed plane of the sketch pad. I broke the oversharpened pencil point almost immediately, trying to enter the paper and scoop into a third dimension; and yet three would have fallen almost as short. I unzipped the huge crushed-velvet pillow of the blue couch in the living room (where my sister and I sat drawing, and where years later, when I was at Eastman, I once lay for four days, banging a tuning fork against my knee and jamming it into my ear and letting the impersonal, stewardessian purity of the A die away until I wasn't sure if I was hearing it or recreating it, in order to force absolute pitch on myself, while I

thought about the machine that had crushed the velvet hard
enough to leave the permanent wrinkles in which my face was
buried) and I slid my hand into a permanently cool place, but was
unenlightened: my hand wasn't really in the pillow at all, but
merely between the inside of the velvet covering and the muslin
of an inner pillow filled with stuffing. My sister was drawing a
picture of a recognizable pillow on a bed, with nice pillowcase
wrinkles and a wedge cut out of it to show the cross section of
messy feathers, like the picture of the earth's inner layers in *The
World We Live In.* Jealously, I wanted to do more than this, yet all
I could show thus far were a few light marks on my page and a tiny
gap where I had broken the pencil point. I thought of what the
drawing ought to look like: some sort of mass of loops, or a
Mercator projection of the interior of that mass; the record of the
pencil's tactile encounter with every feather and inner boundary
as my wrist oriented it in various directions. I needed to catch in
the sketch some of the sensation of reaching inside a new chicken
and pulling out the giblets; or of reaching into the dryer to pull
out hot clothes; or of scraping the seeds from a melon or pulling
the cheap gift out from the bottom of a box of Rice Krispies; or of
plunging a knife into a new jar of peanut butter and creating
complex comma-shaped hollows as you brought a gob of deeper
butter up on the end of the blade. "Stop squirting," my sister said
absently, carefully erasing some small slipup of her realism. I
stopped—I had been using my tongue to shoot tiny packets of
saliva in fast meditative triplets around the roof of my mouth. The
inside of a pillow! To force myself into the proper mental state, I
tried to draw my mouth from my tongue's point of view, hoping to
convey my tongue's persistently mistaken notion that the teeth
formed two complete circles. What I drew resembled a balled-up

55

piece of paper. Finally, defeated, knowing I was cheating, I sketched a primitive pair of lungs, resembling the ones in the ad for Primatene Mist, and an arrow pointing to them that said "From a pillow"; for, as I explained to my mother, the only way to know the real nature of the inside of a pillow was to breathe in its air.

8

THE BUG HERSELF never used pillows, except that time on the plane, when we put one of the miniature ones handed out by the flight attendant on my lap, under her knees. Normally, in her crib, she napped on her back with her fists resting near her ears; if she was startled by a noise in her sleep (a tripped-over cheese grater, for example), she would promptly lift her zipper-blanketed legs vertically in the air like a parking-lot gate and then let them fall, a movement surprisingly reminiscent of my father's way of abruptly raising his head from sleep on the blue couch, falsely alerted by a ringing telephone on the sound track of *The Man from U.N.C.L.E.*, asking a sharp, frowning, nonsensical question— "Have we got all the internegatives from Lenny?"—and then slumping back on the pillow. (As he slept, fortunes in change trickled from his pockets into the couch.) On mornings when Patty got up earlier than I did to feed the Bug, I found that it was extremely pleasant to move my head from my own pillow over to hers for my last twenty minutes in the bed—my diagonal orientation, and the faintly novel saddle shape of her pillow's depression drew me into an unusual pointed form of sleep whose epicenter seemed to be way out on the bridge of my nose. Hers was the very pillow that we had taken with us to pregnancy class to use during breathing exercises; indeed, it was the same pillow we had taken to the hospital, where Patty panted into it, "What was that woman talking about? Those . . . breathing exercises were a total waste . . . worthless . . . useless . . ." It went much better after some Stadol was dripped into her catheter, although then she hallucinated that she was pushing a pile of neatly folded laundry through her cervix. One evening, as with my eyes closed I listened to her write about the Bug, propped up against this same pillow, I thought I could detect the particular sound of a comma just before a pause in her penmanship, but in place of the simple ear shape that she would have made to indicate the punctuational symbol, I visualized the enormous, elaborately typographical commas that my horn professor at the Eastman School, Mal Green, had drawn on Chiarnovsky études that I was working on (using a pencil that otherwise swung distractingly on a string tied to the armature of the music stand) to indicate each place where I should take a breath, for he felt that you were lost unless you breathed identically every time you practiced an excerpt or an étude—and I remembered the time when Mal didn't think I was practicing hard enough and said at one lesson, "You know what? I'm just wondering. This étude is entirely staccato. The whole purpose of it is to get you to make staccato sixteenth notes of perfect regularity. When I think about it, I really wonder if there is any place to breathe in it at all. What do you think?" I nodded uncertainly, and he erased the lifesaving comma he had previously marked on the fourth stave and told me that when I played it for him the next week, I would do the whole thing in one breath. The week passed in a state of hyperventilated mania. I filled my mind with images of bullfrog pouches, bagpipes, dolphin blow-holes, the surplus neoprene meteorological balloons that were advertised in the back of *Popular Science*, the floating spheres in toilet tanks, and the children's book about the Chinese kid who inhaled the sea. The metronome never rested. I developed a strange full feeling at the base of my skull. The étude took only a hundred seconds to play—three hundred and some sixteenth notes. It should have been easy! After all, I had held my breath for over two minutes in fourth-grade lunch hours with Jim Heydemann and Arthur Glasheen: *Sea Hunt* was on every day after school, in which Lloyd Bridges routinely held his breath for incredible stretches while performing heroisms; Jacques Cousteau's first special, about the undersea platform whose inhabitants breathed special mixtures of gases, heavy on the helium and nitrogen, in order to acclimate themselves to life three hundred feet down, was a recent memory; Jim and I had read 20,000 *Leagues Under the Sea* in third grade (Mrs. Nesmith told me that the small Victorian type—Bodoni—would ruin our eyesight), and *Voyage to the Bottom of the Sea* began that season, I think; and we had read an article in *Reader's Digest* that described the sealed letter that Houdini had left to be opened years from then that would explain the secrets of all his tricks, including the one in which he was thrown in the water straitjacketed and locked in a small chest—so feats of breathing were more important to us than anything else that year. And given the paper lunch bags themselves, which you could blow up and make explode, or use to catch an imaginary penny flipped high in the air by snapping the fingers that held the bag to fake the landing, not to mention the newly introduced and highly inspirational plastic sandwich bags, which held their inflation better than paper or wax bags and thus caused a sharper pop, it was not surprising that after the five minutes it took us to eat our lunch we devoted the rest of the half hour to breath-holding experimentation. We filled our chests like cartoon versions of the wolf that blew the pigs' houses down, three of us at once, and then sealed our long-term stores of air behind closed throats as the second hand passed the twelve: we stared at each other, unsmiling, with expressions of puffed, flushed seriousness. The clock hand fell viscously to the twenty mark, the thirty mark. I sucked in my cheeks and made my lips work like Tweety-bird in order to make Art Glasheen snort out a laugh and disqualify himself, but he was unmoved: he turned toward Jim Heydemann and pretended to stun himself with a two-finger poke in the eyeballs; Jim Heydemann, smarter and gentler and less confident than Art Glasheen, couldn't control himself and exhaled suddenly to laugh, involuntarily blowing his nose on his sweater. I used my emergency technique to keep from laughing at Jim's humiliation, turning quickly away and closing my eyes and summoning the worst thing I could remember, or at least one of the worst: not the time I stole fifty cents from my mother's purse, which was too shameful to use as an antisnort device, but a later time when my father took me to the Carnival of Steam, an exhibit of antique farm machinery, to make a sixteen-millimeter film of it, and entrusted me with the rented tape recorder: after a long stretch of filming, including a funny interview with the old woman with cigarette butts in her ears who played the steam calliope, I looked into the plastic window of the tape recorder to see how much recording time we had left and saw, not two neatly turning reels, but a liquid tangle of brown tape churning like clothes in a front-loading washing machine—a stretch of unique time wrinkled, twisted, irretrievably ruined. This sad memory helped keep me in the running. At forty-five seconds Art waved good-bye and put his head on his forearms, and I followed his example: the idea (my idea, in fact—Art Glasheen stole it from *me!*) was that even the act of holding your head upright used oxygen you needed for the two-minute feat and that if you lay on the desk with every muscle relaxed, looking only at the stripes of your shirtsleeve and allowing them to unfocus and split and then slidingly superimpose themselves on each other in false overlayments, you would survive longer, since the focusing was distracting and the corneal muscles involved were too tiny to demand any oxygen themselves. (This optical effect carried over into hypnotic morning sessions with the diamond pattern of the brass hot-air register in the wall near my bed, and the grid of window screens later in the day; and in college I rediscovered it while staring at my Olivetti keyboard trying to finish a senior paper on the use of the word "brain" in Emily Dickinson: as I tried to think of a way to incorporate the folktale cited in the Stith Thompson index in which a god inserts his nose in someone's ear and sucks out his brains, the letters in the middle of the keyboard that were unobscured by my hands would first expand and fuzz out of focus and begin to slide horizontally over each other, and would then lock and resharpen in a mistaken stereotypical space an inch above the real keyboard, the T and Y forming a new hybrid character that resembled a more realistic roadside power-line pole than either letter did individually.) Assuming the role of coach to save face, Jim Heydemann called out the one-minute mark. I let a little air slip out, because by that point it helped to have less poison pressure in the lungs. At about one minute and thirty-five seconds, instinctive futile diaphragm spasms began. I sat up, pounding a crumpled lunch bag on the desk. I snuffed out more bad air. Art Glasheen was rocking back and forth, the tendons of his neck rhythmically sucked into relief as his lungs tried to breathe and weren't allowed to. The instant Jim Heydemann called out

"Two!" we both gasped with genuine desperation. Each lunch hour that we crossed the two-minute mark this way, it became harder, not easier, to accomplish. My father warned me about the dementia suffered by pearl divers, and when I got an A minus for a report on "Getting Rid of Pollution" (my plan involved lots of "great vats" in deserts) I attributed the evil minus sign to breath-holding and told Jim and Art I was quitting. Soon after, my parents gave a huge party (*six* cans of Sterno), at which my job was to operate the hand control for a Kodak carousel slide projector filled with eighty black-and-white slides, all intentionally unidentified and in random order, which my father had shot from ancestral portraits and baby pictures and grandparental daguerreotypes contributed by many of the guests a few days earlier. There was no screen and the lights weren't dimmed: the slides appeared on the blue living room wall as the guests flowed around, yakking and chewing and shouting. A grad student from Eastman had been hired to play requests at the piano, and did the themes from *The Shadow* and *Perry Mason* and, when I asked him later, *Sea Hunt*; in the front hall was a table on which there was a yo-yo, in case one of my father's associates could be persuaded to show off the tricks that had made him state champion, and a deck of cards and juggling balls and a pile of quarters along with a pamphlet on coin tricks by T. Nelson Downs, King of Coins, so that my father could prestidigitate if people seemed interested. A guy who made scissors-silhouette portraits was in the dining room snipping with a peaceful smile next to the fondue trays. I was very proud of my parents, who understood, it seemed to me, that a party had to have *exhibits*, like Expo 67 or science museums, rather than just clumps of people wearing ceramic necklaces and rocking with laughter. At first I didn't know how long I should let each slide stay up, and (feeling overserious in a new sweater) tried to keep to a regimental click-two-three-four rhythm, but as the guests wandered up to the warm projector and started exclaiming, "Albert, is that *you?*" and "Isn't that a scream!" and "Who are *those* sinister slutty young women?" I began to get a feel for it: you shouldn't wait until all the incredulity and laughter for a given shot had died away entirely; instead, you wanted to trigger the cardboard slide's little layup into its berth in the carousel and the drop of the next (a sound like a coin in a pay phone) a little before that moment, because some of it was in fact filler or coattail incredulity, meant simply to congratulate people for earlier funny comments and demonstrate carefree participation until a new slide came on— people wanted to have the image snatched away from them, and they wanted sometimes to shout, "Wait, wait go back to that earlier one with the fake waterfall!" I loved how the living room wall contributed its own blue texture to the graininess of the old photographs, and how the automatic focuser of the slide machine automatically corrected for the buckling of the slide as it fell into the hot white path of light with an HO-scale locomotive sound, and how all those differently sized pictures, some framed, some curling, some cardboard-backed, had been regularized by my father's camera (on a tripod in the basement) to fit in this modern machine. The picture of my father at six months looking cross-eyed and wild-haired on a blanket near a bush, and the one of my mother naked at four on a beach, came around and around, but mixed in with all these other families and their mildly colorful histories my parents caused only average exclamations and were seldom recognized, though I gave them a few seconds longer on the wall—inwardly I was shouting, "Hey, that's my mother who just clicked on! That's my father! These are the people who bought the Sterno for you and waxed the floors and hired the

pianist and set up the projector and are directly responsible for
your shouts and drunken confidences and chummy hands on
shoulders!" I watched a man slide close behind a woman at an
hors d'oeuvres table: as he came in line with her ass he smirkingly
humped against it, jogging her piece of broccoli in the dip (raw
broccoli had just come in that year); I was disgusted and wanted to
take her in my arms and comfort her, but she looked up with only
slight annoyance, or perhaps even with flirtatious pleasure, and
laughed and said, "Pardon *me*, Henry!" At midnight my father
excitedly beckoned everyone toward the stairs; I put the slide
projector on automatic advance so that it would continue to click
away without me, and as the entire party raised a roar of trium-
phant surprise, Brian Blum, a professor of chemistry at the
University of Rochester, slowly descended dressed in a morning
coat and playing an amazingly loud plaid bagpipe. He frowned
and took huge breaths just as Art Glasheen and Jim Heydemann
and I had, but the outcome—a droned blast of a tune that
sounded like "The Ants Go Marching Two by Two" was far more
impressive than our two-minute breath-holding; and sometimes
he took his mouth from the instrument and shouted "Yee-haw!"
and yet because of the reserves of air in the third lung of the
bagpipe itself that he squeezed under his elbow, the piping continued in full force. The next day I told my father I had to learn
the bagpipes; he said that I might want to "build my wind" by
starting out on the French horn, and he told me about Dennis
Brain, the virtuoso of the Mozart concerti who was killed in a car
accident at the height of his powers. The name Brain appealed to
me, so I rented a public-school horn to prepare myself for the
bagpipes, and as a result nine years later, a freshman at Eastman,
I was still playing it, still performing feats of oxygen deprivation,
in order to prepare a Chiarnovsky étude that Mal Green capri-

ciously thought ought to be done in a single breath; yet this time it was harder, of course, because all evidence of strain was forbidden: and at the next lesson, as I took a long covert breath and began playing from memory, staring at the dangling pencil, and made it past the place where Mal had erased the breath comma, I thought of those public-TV ballet specials at the end of which you saw the dancers happily bowing and smiling and gesturing archly to each other in tribute, but then you noticed when you looked more carefully that their little starved stomachs were madly inhaling under their swan feathers, rabbit-panting, and you realized in a burst of pity for squandered lives of physical practice that all they really wanted to do was to take big replenishing gasps and stand bent over with their hands on their knees, shaking their heads and saying, "Whoo!—man oh man am I beat!" but instead they had to hold these ventriloquist's smiles until the curtain fell. By the last measure of the étude I had no air left in me, but I forced the final notes out anyway, crushing some residual foam from my alveoli. I expected my breastbone to snap like a Popsicle stick—and all for a piece of late-Romantic academicism by Chiarnovsky! Mal switched off the metronome and nodded and said, "All right, it's physically possible." Then he took the pencil and put back the comma on the fourth stave—a beautiful, deliberate, dark comma!—and told me to get a drink of water and play it for him again. I did, and I experienced some of the purged, post-throwup happiness he meant me to feel, but in the weeks that followed I felt a growing disgust with the French horn's third-grade-level subjection to bodily mechanics, and I decided to transfer to Swarthmore and spend my time reading prose and writing papers, where commas could be stuck in and taken out without the risk of physical injury.

9

EVEN SO, when Patty's handwriting paused for a moment that evening soon after the Bug was born, and I held in my mind a tiny pen-sound that I felt sure was a comma, I didn't at first think of literary punctuation at all, but of the distant preliterate sight of Mal Green's markings on my horn études. The idea of the comma as an oasis of respiration, a point of real as opposed to grammatical breath, of momentary renewal and self-marshaling in the dotty onslaught of sixteenth notes, overlaid itself on my idea of the comma as a unit of simple disjunction in written English. How had we come up with this civilized shape? I wondered. Timidly and respectfully it cupped the sense of a preceding phrase and held it out to us. It recalled the pedals of grand pianos, mosquito larvae, paisleys, adult nostril openings, the spiraling decays of fundamental particles, the prows of gondolas, half-spent tubes of antifungal ointment, falcon or airplane wings in cross section: there was an implied high culture in its asymmetrical tapering swerve that gave it a distinct superiority over the Euclidean austerity of the full point, or period. You

might in fact have expected these two elements of disjun
exhibit reversed functions: the comma seems more of a foi
progress of the eye, a fallen branch partially impeding a stream,
while the period, a mere dot, a small cold pebble, should allow
sense to slip smoothly past. But perhaps the functions were as they
were, I thought, because the graceful purling motion necessary to
the creation of the comma, that inclusive flip of the pen, is
similar to the motions we use in writing the prose that surrounds
it, while the period is an alien jab, tacking the sentence with
finality onto the paper. Even after Aldus Manutius put his type-
casters to work, and they resolved the informal kinetics of its
written formation into theoretically sound protractor-twirls and
conic sections, the comma still retained all its original expressive-
ness, miming the extenuating dips of the hand we use when
taking exception to a point in polite conversation. And in those
recent typefaces in which commas have been chamfered into
little more than rude cuneiformal wedges, their newer shape
nonetheless manages at least to evoke the rubber doorstop's de-
pendable amenity, keeping the ostioles free from clause to clause,
allowing metaphors to mix more freely. Working myself up into a
state of reverence as I lay there, I began to be curious whether the
statistical ratio of commas to sentences might have a predictive
use in some sort of moral stylometrics: maybe, as a general rule,
the fewer commas a person used, the more ruthless a tyrant he
would prove to be if placed in a position of power. It was a test that
would itself be useful to the tyrannically minded, and it was
worthless besides, as I realized only a few seconds later, remem-
bering for the fiftieth time a 1975 Thanksgiving vacation after I
had transferred to Swarthmore, during which I made my mother
cry by too sharply criticizing her use of a comma before a
parenthesis in a letter she was writing to the op-ed page of the

Times-Union opposing the reelection of a certain family court judge. Made panicky by several bad grades on papers, I had tried to catch up on prose composition that semester, and as a result I came home that Thanksgiving filled with evil little ordinances from Sheridan Baker and *Words into Type* and Strunk & White and that big orange hog-butcher-of-the-world *Manual of Style*. Instead of praising her letter's force and rightness, I said, "Mom, you've got to get a grip on how to handle commas—you leave them out on one side of a clause, and right here you use a comma before *paren along with future catastrophes of judgment we can't begin to foresee close paren!*"

"Why is that wrong?"

"Because a comma always comes *after* the paren. And you do it again here as well. And here!" I, an illiterate ex-horn player, was telling *her*, who had spontaneously recited Frost's "Desert Places" and Shelley's "Ozymandias" to us on the beach in Bermuda, who had lavished praise on my second-grade essay about garbagemen that had no commas at all and capitalized the first letter of every noun and used a ditto sign each time a word coincidentally appeared below itself on a line, who all through my years of high school, which I spent playing Wff'n Proof badly and listening to *La Mer* and planning symphonies I never wrote, kept saying hopefully, "You know, Mike, those nineteenth-century novels really aren't too bad—they move slowly, because people had more time to read then, but they take hold of you—you might give the old *Moonstone* a try to start with"—I was telling *her* off about matters of literary convention? When I saw her bow her head over the letter to the op-ed page and then actually make a sound that I realized after a moment of bewilderment was a sob, I was shocked. "Mom! No! It was just a critique! I didn't mean it in a bad way!"

She said, "This is nothing, Mike, I appreciate your comments, it just hit me wrong, don't worry about this, I'm fine. *It's just so hard to say the shitty little thing I need to say!*" She sobbed again.

I handed her a paper towel. If a sensitivity to the disposition of the comma was a sign of humanity, how could I have been so inhuman as to make my mother cry in this way? It might have been that I was harsh simply because I was startled: I had expected as a matter of course that she, who stood for the literate side of my upbringing, as my father stood for the musical side, would know by instinct every modern rule and prohibition of punctuation. I knew her spelling was uncertain, of course—but I thought her "immagination" and "seperate" and "ellephant" were bits of colorful camouflage that her brain cleverly hid behind, so that her intelligence would inspire affection rather than jealousy; and when Mrs. Nesmith, my third-grade teacher, once sneeringly circled "exqused" on a note my mother had hastily written for me, I felt a greater pointedness of dislike toward that rouged and girdled witch than when she ridiculed my Beatle haircut or told Jim Heydemann and me that we would go blind reading Jules Verne. I had had years to adjust to and explain and defend my mother's quirks of spelling to myself, so that when I met Patty two years later, and found that *her* spelling was as shaky as my mother's, I felt I understood this weakness immediately, and I was able to comfort her with an unusual intensity of conviction when she got papers back with outraged underlines below "amoung" and "begining" and with notes saying, "Your argument is spirited and nicely phrased, but your spelling is atrocious. *Write with the dictionary beside you.*" She may even have begun to love me not when I stuck nickels in my nose for a cheap laugh or when I announced to a dorm-roomful of freshwomen that my genitalia were constructed on a humble scale and they ought to know this about me and judge their actions accordingly (feeling in the seconds before I made this statement the wild throaty feeling of intending to say something adventurous), but rather when I sat beside her one afternoon on her bunk bed after she had gotten a history paper back and reassured her and stroked her arm and made cutting remarks about French academies and low-synonym-count Romance languages in general and then talked about the tribute bad spelling paid to the essential disorder and mixtion of our language—that imperfect linkage between aural and visual images that made ideas like *through* and *heart* blur and rise so ungrudgingly off the page and into an ampler mental dimension several inches above it, and then told her my terrible story of coming in second in the spelling bee in second grade by spelling *keep* "c-e-e-p" after successfully tossing off *microphone*, and how for two or three years afterward I was pained every time a yellow garbage truck drove by on Highland Avenue and I saw the capitals printed on it, "Help Keep Our City Clean," with that impossible irrational K that had made me lose so humiliatingly with a one-syllable word. But my mother's informal punctuation in the op-ed letter came as a complete surprise; and the fact that my immediate instinctive response to it was to point out the misplaced commas so harshly that she wept (the only time, as far as I remember, that I ever hurt her feelings—for she understood and was even amused by my teenage request that whenever the two of us walked down the street together, she would please walk at least three yards ahead of me, so that people wouldn't know we were related; and she even played along in her compliance, whistling, walking with a theatrical solitariness, checking her pocketbook, pausing abruptly to glance at a window display), as if these faulty commas called into question our standing as a family—the fact that I had been instinctively so cruel, made me double up with misery when, after I was married, I came across some sentences in Boswell that were punctuated *just as hers had been*. Boswell (and De Quincey, Edward Young, and others) had treated the sunken garden of a parenthetical phrase just as my mother had—as something to be prepared for and followed by the transitional rounding and softening of a comma. And such hybrids—of comma and parenthesis, or of semicolon and parenthesis, too—might at least in some cases allow for finer calibrations between phrases, subtler subordinations, irregular varieties of exuberance and magisteriality and fragile conjunction. In our desire for provincial correctness and holy-sounding simplicity and the rapid teachability of intern copy editors we had illegalized all variant forms—and, as with the loss of subvarieties of corn or apples, this homogenization of product was accomplished at a major unforeseen cost: our stiff-jointed prose was less able, so I now huffily thought, full of vengeance against the wrong I had done my mother, to adapt itself to those very novelties of social and technological life whose careful interpretation and weighing was the principal reason for the continued indispensability of the longer sentence. We even repunctuated the past, further destroying the genetic fund of replenishing counterexample and idiosyncratic usage. For instance, as I had recently discovered, Dero Saunders, the editor of the Viking *Portable Gibbon*, willfully removed numerous commas:

> In addition, I have also taken the liberty of repunctuating and reparagraphing Gibbon throughout. By today's standards, a reader would have every right to complain that Gibbon used too much punctuation and too few paragraphs. (*The Portable Gibbon*, editor's intro., p. 23.)

And M. A. Stewart even more radically reprocesses Robert Boyle:

71

My greatest departures are in punctuation, since the significance of different kinds of pointing has changed considerably since Boyle's day. I have not therefore tried to take Boyle's punctuation as a base and then merely tinker with it, since that seemed the least likely way to achieve reasonable consistency of practice. I have repointed from scratch, conscious of the need to give a clear lead as to the general structure of Boyle's convoluted periods, and to make his prose *flow* as naturally for a twentieth-century reader as the archaisms in vocabulary and syntax will permit. Even by seventeenth-century standards, Boyle was a poor stylist, too much given to weak cadences. (M. A. Stewart, *Selected Philosophical Papers of Robert Boyle*, pp. xxvi–xxvii.)

Imagine this guy Stewart talking about *flow* to the magnificent Boyle, the first man to understand the nature of air! Crazed degenerate! Yet was I doing anything to correct these wrongs? I was idle. Thinking over Mal Green and my mother as I lay next to Patty, I began to contemplate writing some sort of concentrated history of the comma—not a history of all of punctuation, for that would be much too ambitious—but one of those appealing little monographs published by Cambridge, Nelson, Routledge, or Butterworth that the hand reaches for in libraries between the huge American-bound books on either side, not necessarily because the American books will claim too much and fail to stay pliantly allusive in their comprehensiveness and show little sensitivity to the civilizing power of the comma, although they may do these things, but simply because the spines of the British books are covered in a finer-woven blue or red or green cloth, as smooth as a not perfectly clean pillowcase, and seem as a result able to submit to the impress of the gold stamping of the title and author with more exactitude than the coarser textile American publishers use almost without exception. A short history of the comma, then, that would attempt to hold the library of written prose superimposedly up to a light bulb, so that one or more tiny routes would reveal themselves, as in a stack of punch cards, passing through all the stomata of individual commas directly back to the original point of momentary breath-held stillness between two phrases. Of course I would have to read up on paleography. I might even have to learn some Latin. But at least it would be for a good cause. I saw myself looking up old printers' manuals, or snagging a fellowship at Dumbarton Oaks to study the failed attempts by Byzantine lexicographers to impose various systems of high, middle, and low marks on lines of manuscript that indicated values of pause (I'd have to get some Greek going, too); I'd check into Carolingian breath marks and the disappearance of the virgule, and maybe I'd tour colometry, seeing what I could make of conventions of scribal payment and their incentive to reduce the numbers of pages by the removal of interword spaces, and the muting effect of whole phrase-spacing in turn on the need for graphical punctuation; and then I'd glance at the growth of sophisticated conventions of abbreviation and their suppression of the full potential of a simultaneously comprehensible system of disjunction that relied on the same symbols. Self-taught? *Pencil neck?* They wouldn't even know what pencil neck was until I ramped up and began a course of concentrated reading more fanatically comprehensive even than De Quincey's eighteen-hour-a-day burst at Oxford before the exam he ran away from into a life of enforced journalism! I would out-page- and out-scroll-flip Accursius, who, hearing that a rival scholar, Odofred, was occupied with a redaction of the extant versions of the Code of Justinian that would overlap the huge *Glossa Ordinaria* on which he, Accursius, was at work, feigned illness, turned away his students, and in a cackling seclusion completed his massive task in "barbarous Latin"! I'd charge past Porson, who, raised in a remote cottage with only three or four books to consult, supplemented with random volumes of Chamber's *Cyclopædia* washed ashore from a shipwreck, developed himself into an effortlessly erudite drunk, able to shoot off a four-hundred-page proslogium defending Gibbon's assertion that a certain verse in St. John's First Epistle was spurious, against the counterattack of an unsuspecting archdeacon! In five years of the most consuming solitary study, like the scholar my mother liked so much in *Mistress Masham's Repose* who lived on nothing but tea, or Old Doctor Wango Tango, who subsisted on scraps of bread and eventually was blown away in a high wind along with his bony pets, or like the Quangle Wangle Quee, living the life of the mind in a tree, wearing a hat even bigger than the "formidable" one Bentley used while immersed in his philological emendations to shade his eyes, I would remove myself from the world and cross-index with fearsome single-mindedness in order to arrive at an overwhelming burden of evidence to support my nonsensical contention that the refinement of the comma, increasingly assuming the phrasally organizing functions performed by word endings in the highly inflected languages, made vernacular prose possible— that the comma, in short, was alone responsible for the passage of civilization north from the ancient world into the modern. But of course I had a family; I had a Bug to take care of; instead of reading journals of paleography, I lay awake listening to my wife write in felt-tip pen in her journal; any sort of furious antiquarianism was impossible in this lulling domestic setting. And yet other scholars did it! Isaac Casaubon, for instance, one of the most compulsive polyhistors of all time, bent with study, according to Scaliger, had spared time to raise, or at least father, a child—the same Casaubon who in 1614, even as he was dying of the strain of years of "unintermitted study" and of complications of a congenitally deformed dual bladder, which, like a bagpipe, boasted (so the post mortem revealed) a secondary storage area in which painful calculi formed amidst a general purulence, in part caused by his chronic "inattention to the calls of nature, while the mind of the student was engaged in study and contemplation" (as Mark Pattison, his nineteenth-century biographer, tactfully has it), and which calculi became when I read about them the emblems of learnedness without sufficient issue, knowledge that wasn't whizzed out but retained to the point of internal damage within the knower—this man who, even as his bladder's expanding sidecar was killing him, worked harder than ever on his ambitious (so I'd heard) refutation of the *Annales Ecclesiastici* of Baronius, in which he proved by textual evidence that the corpus of hermetic writings which people had long wanted to believe was the work of an Egyptian scribe, Hermes Trismegistus, or Thoth, were in fact much later, early Christian, and that therefore the alchemical seal of Hermes, or hermetic seal (a closure which apparently required the actual melting shut of the glass aperture through which the ingredients were poured into the retort, so that the interior contents become a separate world, with its own atmospheric effects of fluxion and refluxion and calcination, and which lent its ancient and flavorful name to the airtight screw-on luting of the much later jars of peanut butter, giving that inert and base and untransmutable golden oily material some of the proto-scientific alchemical romance of elixirs and iatrochemical concoctions "hermetically sealed" for weeks and months until they morphosed themselves into substances of unknown but surely powerful efficacy)—that this Seal of Hermes Trismegistus (himself an acknowledged inspiration to aspiring scholiasts such as Burton or Milton who wanted, as I momentarily did, to seal themselves away for a time and read every waking moment in order to hold within them, like the huge-headed Chinese kid who inhaled the sea, enough of the written past that their own thoughts would merge and react with and dissolve into it, so that what they wrote would be a record not of a single life but of all life, and hence epical) owed its thrice magnificent name to some early Christian writer who, so Casaubon's killing labors proved, thought his own thoughts weren't sufficient by themselves and craved the hieratic grandeur of ancient sources enough to pretend that what came from his pen was a millennium older than it was. Surely, with Casaubon as my example, I could compile a short but leadenly dense philology of the comma, despite social obligations, marital requirements, and days when I had the Bug to take care of. The notion made my heart nudge me with powerful, ambitious arrhythmias, and as Patty put her spiral notebook on the floor and turned out her light, I imagined myself at scholarly gatherings, aloof, Boo Radley shy, a shirttail untucked, politely not taking notice as people whispered and pointed at me: "See that guy there with the terrible posture? He's the world's authority on the comma! He's studied the negative spaces in prose for twenty-eight years! He sees the comma as the embodiment of civilization, as the true 'volute' in 'evolution'; he's tried to focus all of humane letters into that tiny curlicue. Can you believe it? Fruitcake!" But no, I thought, my horn professor's commas, my mother's commas, Patty's notebook commas were the only episodes in the history of punctuation that I would ever know enough about to speak with authority: except, of course, for the Bug herself, whose shape—big head, tapering extremities— when I first saw it glowing indistinctly on the ultrasound screen, and when I later hugged her real bent self to me, had introduced a quiet, golden, shade-pulled moment of retrospective suspension in my life that elevated the whole undistinguished serial succession of years that preceded it into something that made sense, something with the unity and introductory springiness of the first clause in a complex sentence. The breathing Bug was civilizing me; she was my comma.

In the darkness, Patty whispered something. (We had gotten into the habit of whispering because of the light-sleeping Bug in the next room—and I had been interested to notice that the unvoiced passage of air through the vocal chords actually tired them and dried them out more, although the volume of sound was much less, than speaking in normal tones.) She said, "Excuse me—Fatboy? You're *breathing* very strangely. You sound as if you're smoking a pipe. Are you all right?"

I froze.

.... .10. . . . .

I FROZE, I didn't answer immediately, because as I had been thinking with increasing excitement about becoming a learned man in order to write a history of the comma, I had been picking my nose, an act I had believed I could perform silently; but as I had continued to pick away I had evidently been making a series of tiny "Ah!" sounds by closing and opening my vocal apparatus, releasing short breaths, and these were what Patty had heard. In nearly all cultures nose-picking is considered a disgusting habit, and I debated whether I should tell her the truth straight out or merely apologize and murmur something plausible about not being able to get that "Ah!"-filled section of the radio oldie that goes, "What's your name, who's your daddy," etc. out of my head. The two of us often used unsavory physical revelations to test adoration's power to absorb and transform the crudest provisions into lovable and revealing things about each other. For instance, when we got engaged, we had already been "sexing," as Patty called it, for years, since college, so on the first morning after she accepted the ring, instinctively sensing that we had to find some further upward cranking of intimacy that would celebrate our newly permanized relationship, she got out of the hotel bed and, indicating the bathroom with her thumb, bravely said, "Excuse me for a moment, Changlibore. I have to, I need to go *big job.*" Of course we had each been vaguely aware of intervals before that moment when the other had disappeared into the bathroom and then reappeared with a slightly uneasy look, and we may even have occasionally spoken of the act of "number two," but Patty's forthright statement, using an idiom that was quite new to me, which she said she had learned visiting friends once in Minnesota (and in that offering of novelty supplying another instance of why I needed her in my life), held the thrilling promise that now that we were engaged, we would be in no doubt about the specific purpose of our trips to the bathroom. From then on we preannounced our *big jobs* more and more; and if Patty rattled the bathroom door and I called warningly out from inside, "Um! I'm in the middle of something very 'big,' baby," she would mock-casually ask, "Jobbing, eh?" and I would reply, mock-sheepishly, "I'm afraid I am."

"Pain?"

"Some."

"Grunt it out and you'll be fine."

Our intimacy didn't extend, ever, to jobbing in each other's immediate presence, and only in emergencies was one person allowed to job while the other was in the shower, but aside from that tasteful limit, any frankness seemed possible. In the months that followed, she told me how she often rushed around the apartment looking for just the right thing to flip through while she jobbed, rejecting the book or magazine she had been reading in favor of some other, often a specialized work of reference— Beal's *Grasses of North America,* for instance. That's kind of incredible, I told her—I did the same thing! Sometimes I spent four or five minutes hurriedly scanning my bookcases, wanting something I hadn't examined in a long time, something out of the way, improving, life-advancing, lamp-smelling, *jobworthy,* so that this tiresome physical act would be a step forward, although by the time I finally sat down with a volume of my grandfather's 1911 *Encyclopædia Britannica* I barely had time to locate an article on Accursius or Porson and read one sentence before I was done and could reshelve the book and resume whatever real reading I had been in the midst of. And while a certain class of books, difficult to define, was proper accompaniment *for* jobbing, other publications, Patty confided, especially coffee-table compilations about interior decoration and white-sale circulars, inevitably *brought on* a sharp need to job; and I told her about my similar problem in libraries: almost the minute I walked into the stacks bearing slips of paper with Library of Congress numbers scribbled on them, even before I had located a single book, I had to start looking around for the arrows to the bathroom. Nor was this instant demand caused by some psychological trigger having to do with literature, for it had been just as true when I had browsed in the Sibley Music Library at Eastman, looking for chamber music with interesting horn parts or miniature scores of *La Mer* and *The Miraculous Mandarin,* as when I had sought out concordances at Swarthmore's library to see whether Tennyson or Milton had ever used the word "brain" in the ways Emily Dickinson had, or as later when I got within noseshot of the patent records in MIT's Barker Library while looking up a reference to the aerodynamics of smokestacks. New books, and bookstores, had no effect on me. After years of experiencing this nuisance, mentioning it to nobody, I finally ascribed it to some specific component of book dust or binder's glue and became resigned to it (as I became resigned to the way two cups of coffee would always bring on, along with mental clarity, a ten-minute burst of sneezing and runny nose)—and now, in Patty, after all these years, I had found someone who was willing to listen to me talk about it!

There was so *much* to share. If we both coincidentally arrived at the bathroom at the same time, we would shake our heads sadly, each deferring to the other and saying what a regular "jobber's fiesta" it was today. Once Patty tried to remember if she had already gone big job that morning or not and was unable to, and lamented her case of "jobanesia"; and from then on, if one of us had to go out of town for some reason, the observation we used over the phone as proof of how much we missed each other was the mention of the total jobanesia we had suffered because nobody had been around to inquire about or describe each daily manifestation to, making it stick in memory. When Ford ads came on the TV saying that "Quality is Job 1," we slit our eyes and nodded sagely. I told her about the time my family and I had driven up to Expo 67 in Montreal, and how, because it was the happiest, fullest week of my life so far, I had decided to commemorate its greatness privately by not going big job for the whole seven days we spent there, repeatedly clenching the obtruder back up for further revision; but I made it only to day four. For a time, toward the end of our first year of marriage, I thought "big job" might be losing its freshness between us, and I instead began saying I needed to go "Burmese." But no, "job" was too natural, too useful; it was fated to be the permanent word between us, surviving even the overexposure of parental diaper-changing.

Once, soon after the Bug was born, Patty asked me (apropos of whether we should have another baby and when) if I had ever fantasized when I was small about giving birth, as she had. So I told her how long before adolescence I used to flip through the

photographs in *The Family of Man* in search of the childbirth
sequence, straddling the arm of the blue couch so as to twonk the
buried root of my pointless erection back and forth over its stuffed
shape. I would study the woman's face as it changed from picture
to picture (I thought it was the same woman, but in fact it was
several different women), her tranquil expression as she stood in
front of a window and then her sudden shift to a frowning,
squinting lip-curled physicalness that I found extremely hot: the
benevolence of her pain, the enclosure of what I felt somehow was
a sexual moan in the lust-transfiguring generousness of allowing
a life to pass hurtfully through her widening bones, and the last
vein-poppingly riveting picture before the infant itself was held
above her, combined with what I felt was her loving generosity to
me, the youthful and innocent page-flipper, in allowing herself to
be graphically photographed for this good cause. That she didn't
mean her consent to be sexual, that the editor of *The Family of
Man* didn't mean it to be sexual, made it all the more so;
something that was also true of TAM, the Teaching Automated
Mannikin (or "Talking," or "Totally"?), a life-size transparent
plastic talking woman that was installed at the Rochester Museum & Science Center when I was in fifth grade. It was the
golden age of sex education; an intricate exhibit of turn-of-the-
century glassmaking and lens-grinding techniques, sponsored by
Bausch & Lomb, had apparently been torn out to make way for
this plastic woman—and although I had loved pushing the worn
Bakelite button that made the glass exhibit's motor slowly *oom*
into motion (like a sewing machine whose pedal is so lightly
depressed that at first you hear a hum of pure magnetic urge
without any actual needle movement) more than anything else in
the museum, and I hated the kids who pounded their fists on the
button, causing the miniature glassmaking attendants to move

jerkily in their table-hockey tracks, I forgave the curators for removing it (it ultimately went to the Smithsonian, I think, where it was placed in storage)—since TAM's quasi-robotic nudity was probably almost as alluring a combination for them as it was for me. I read an article about TAM in the *Times-Union* and went in during her first week of operation: with trembling hands I locked my bike to a fence near the museum and found the circular shack upstairs where she was. A sign said "TAM's next show will be at:" and a clock's hands pointed to one-twenty. Her show! In twenty minutes she would with complete kindly mature calmness in the spirit of science and free inquiry show us her organs. I killed time by hurrying past the huge, ragged-clawed, late-Silurian eurypterids in "Rochester's Ancient Seas" so that I would have something to report to my mother. At one-twenty, I followed a group of Camp Fire Girls and a Camp Fire mother who eyed me suspiciously into a small hushed room with carpeting on the walls and on three rows of backless curved pews. Before us, on a pedestal, stood a grown woman in clear plastic, her arms held open, her head thrown back—modeled for the sake of probity on some Samothracian ideal, although her pose reminded me at the time of the beautiful woman in the beginning of the Coke ad who sang "I'd like to teach the world to sing" as she walked toward us, leading a *Family of Man*-type harmonious crowd. She, TAM, was as yet as wholesome, as entirely uncarnal, as a transparent Bic pen, although I thought I could detect molded nipples in the tastefully unpronounced see-through surface bulges of her plastron. But then the lights came down and she started talking. Her mouth didn't move, of course, and her eyes and the features of her face were smoothed and depersonalized, and her unromantic two-cylinder brain was visible behind, but the taped voice—Seven Sisters with a hint of smoker's roughness

83

or bump-it-with-a-trumpet burlesque-hall vocal strain—that came from her part of the chamber was perfectly appropriate for her shape, I thought. She introduced herself. She told us that she was going to tell us about her body. And then she told us about her body: her liver, her muscles, her heart, her various systems—and as she talked she was kind enough to light up the appropriate organs in Rand McNally colors. Her kindness, her unlascivious nudity, and the imminence of the words "my reproductive system," gave me a sharp little pipette of a boner. And then, finally, she said what I had been waiting for: "And these are my breasts." As she said it, two mobcap-shaped areas of what she explained was fatty tissue lit up in white. Jesus God! White had not been used for any other part of her body! This was much better than the tribal woman nursing the two tiny elephants in Heinrich Kley! This was even better than the inch-and-a-half-high reproductions of "Ads We Could Do Without," topless trade-magazine women in front of gigantic pieces of manufacturing equipment, in the back pages of my father's copies of *Advertising Age!* This was better than the thrilling euphemism of the words "the bosom" in a certain bra ad in, I think, *The New York Times Magazine,* or even the charged absence of a direct object at the end of "to lift and separate," in the Cross Your Heart bra ad! "And these are my breasts," she said, in a tone of gentle assurance, wisdom, resignation—as if to imply that, yes, she was aware that she was uncoyly allowing our eyes a long, scorchingly frank look at them, allowing us even to see the spotlit lymphatic structures beneath, because once they were presented to us in this saintly, unfurtive way, in our formative years, all misplaced lusts and irresponsible pregnancies and destructive infidelity would disappear from the world. The Camp Fire Girls filed out; I hovered, but I was too aware of a museum staff person waiting outside to try to touch

TAM's knee. And bicycling home I found that already TAM's knee, her nude immobile physical self, was becoming less interesting than the idea of the real woman who had been paid to do TAM's voice. Even years later I would think of this unknown woman in the recording studio with the script in front of her, leaning very close to the microphone so that every intimate palatal event that accompanied her words was recorded, reading about her innocent spleen or thyroid or skeletal system, and yet thinking as she took her professional breaths at each set of dot-dot-dots that the moment when she would have to say, "And these are my breasts," was coming ever closer: Would she bring out the sentence with the relaxed, full-lipped, mature aplomb that she as a trained and highly paid voice was expected to have, when reading these words was in the world of sound equivalent to standing up in the thickly carpeted room and letting her shirt fall open and holding her arms apart for the instantly tit-maddened audio technicians beyond the glass? Surely the fact that this noble educational project licensed her to use the lipsticked richness of her voice to discourse on the merits of her own breasts and yet remain free of any suspicion that this kind of forthrightly smutty talk was in any sense arousing was itself somewhat arousing to her? Surely after the taping she sped home, posed lazily and cuppingly in front of her mirror, letting a string of heavy plastic beads hook itself on the Milk Dud of a nipple, in a way she hadn't since she was sixteen, and then fell back on the bed and clitted her yum-stump to a box-spring-deep pelvis-lifter of what Patty called an "organasm"? I *know* she did.

And this real woman behind the transparently idealized TAM fused for me with the close-ups of the face of the moaning, grunting, back-arching woman giving birth in *The Family of Man*—We strip, I seemed to hear them both saying, *for a better world*. After twenty minutes of close study of the birthing woman's face, I was excited enough to leave the book on the coffee table and go upstairs to the bathroom and stand in front of the door's mirror puffing out my stomach and running my hands over it as over a crystal ball, imagining the pressure of pushing a whole child through one's crotch. Then, for contrast, I'd suck in my abdominal region so that it was a shocking hollow and tighten the vertical muscle, as I had seen illustrated in a book of yoga-over-forty exercises that my grandmother used; then I took another big breath and plumped out my stomach again, as far as it would go, like the nose cone of a passenger plane, frowning and inflating my cheeks to heighten the effect. Finally it was time to arrange two double-square lengths of toilet paper on the tiled floor to form a small square target, and (only if I knew myself to be sufficiently constipated that I wouldn't make a mess) try, still standing, to labor out a small pebble of job so that it fell onto the toilet paper, while at the same time keeping clearly in mind the good-hearted struggles of the *Family of Man* woman, pretending to wince as she had with selfless pain, tightening all my neck tendons as I pushed with her for this worthy cause. One time, inspired by the elaborate marble shoots that my father and I used to tape together out of paper towel and toilet paper tubes in the alcove, and inspired too by a drawing in Heinrich Kley of a chimp pretending to poop through a king's crown, I tried to job onto the landing pad of the toilet paper *through* a toilet paper tube: interesting until about midway through, when suddenly the whole thing became, as I told Patty, silly and unpleasant and uninteresting and physically *heavy*. I dropped the used tube in the toilet with distaste, flushed and left; half an hour later my mother found me on the back porch, surrounded by plastic models of cars and planes. She was holding a helix of sodden cardboard. "Mike, the toilet was stopped up. Did you do this?"

"Yes." I blushed.

"Okay. Is it something you do often?"

"No."

"Okay. It's okay to do it, just so you don't do it too often."

We never spoke of it again. I abandoned the experiments in pregnancy simulation not long after, and when at Expo 67 I saw brief movie footage, in color, of an actual childbirth—at the Czech pavilion, I think, in a confusing multimedia show in which a number of enormous cube-shaped screens moved forward and backward showing component pieces of larger images—I watched with diminished interest, and didn't connect it at all with my heroic attempt to keep from jobbing for that same whole week. By my senior year of college, I had entirely forgotten the effect that the birth pages in *The Family of Man* had once had on me: I read some snippy comments by Jacques Barzun about the photography book's anti-intellectualism and when my mother chanced to say how much my sister and I had *loved* looking through it when we were small, I dismissed it brusquely as valuing crude feeling over rational thought and Western history and refined moral speculation. It wasn't until Patty began bringing home fancy you-and-your-baby books early in her pregnancy with photographs of women in labor that I again felt stirrings of that odd sort of lustful gratitude that I had once felt so strongly toward the anonymous woman who had allowed her face to become contorted with the self-abandonment of birth while a highbrow photographer clicked away: the "giving" of "giving birth" again became dimly sexual.

.........11........

PATTY HERSELF, WHILE PREGNANT, in a hormone cloud of lust, favored me with candid reports of how on the way to work she sometimes wanted to tear off the clothes of every not-positively-ugly man and woman she saw in the subway car. But I didn't tell *her* about jobbing on squares of toilet paper until after the Bug was born—and even then, as I construed the memory in words for the first time, I wondered uneasily whether I might not be passing some limit beyond which her affection, lacking the pure horsepower necessary to twist an image intrinsically this unpleasant into something lovable, would begin to falter, though she might not sense it then. And this unease in fact was part of the exciting risk of our mutual revelations. Was there a limit between us? Would disgust ever outweigh love? Would the magic of all of our happy chatter about big jobs suddenly disintegrate, and seem not thrillingly intimate but rather uncaring and sloppy, as if we viewed each other no longer as lovers but as indifferent medical personnel, or caretakers to the insane, for whom repugnancies were just part of a day's work? And this pleasing uncertainty returned in full force the night Patty said I sounded as if I were smoking a pipe. Perhaps nose-picking was the very threshold of revulsion beyond which her love for me would begin to sustain damage. Shared urination certainly hadn't undermined it: she happily encircled my urine stream with an A-okay sign made with her index and thumb while I shouted, "Wo, careful, it's beginning to wane, look out!" Why should nose-picking be more objectionable than that? It was true that Patty had no special fond private name to give nose-picking, as she did for jobbing, and the irritating Dennis the Menace snigger of the term itself was not a point in its favor. In addition, jobbing was an act everyone was required to perform, while nose-pickers were considered miserable weak functionaries who could not keep their fiddling fingers from this self-indulgence. It inspired none of the reverence that psychoanalysis reserved for whacking off. And yet in my experience a certain amount of daily maintenance work on the interior of the nose was *necessary*, physically necessary, simply to avoid panicky feelings of claustrophobia, especially in the dry winter months. Those high hardened ridges had to be removed. Once again, it was caring for the Bug that had brought me to the verge of contemplating an admission of my frequent nose efforts to Patty. The Bug's nose cried out to be picked: she would develop colds and breathe great multiphonic bone-flute breaths; and because of the extreme cleanness of her nose, you could see exactly the formation that was causing all the trouble. At first she shook her head as I tried to pick it, but soon she associated the freer breathing she enjoyed afterward with my attentions, and allowed me the half-second it took to thumb away the offending bit of tephra. On a crowded holiday train from New York to Boston around this time I heard two bratty kids and their father embarrass their beleaguered mother by loudly repeating the old joke about

89

how you can pick your friends, and you can pick your nose, but you can't pick your friend's nose. What I thought then was: Ah, but the amazing thing is, you *can* pick your child's nose! Yet what was a cute necessity in an infant might still seem to be a loathsome act in an adult. It probably wouldn't be too hard to tell Patty how for almost the entire stretch of first through sixth grades I had been so revolted by my own mucus when I had a bad cold that I would refuse to blow it out, despite my mother's pleas. "Now Mike, you're faking again. Just blow! Just take a deep breath and really blow!" I would lie through long nights, waiting for a single flooded nostril to clear on its own, or hoping that the air from the brass hot-air register would at least dry it enough for me to get to work on it: and then in my despair I would turn again on my other side and suddenly experience a piercing joyful turpentine feeling as a Northwest Passage through one sinus arrowed open after days of double blockage; repeatedly I thanked evolution for giving us two nostrils, and hence two separate chances to win breath's lottery. But could I tell Patty that even as a grown man I found the inrush of cool air in a well-picked nostril an indisputable joy, and well worth the risk of a nosebleed? There was often a flat plate over the inner septum which, when, unsuccessful in getting a purchase on higher masses, you tried to slide it out, almost always gave you an immediate though easy-to-sniff-dry nosebleed; later that day, an innocent forgetful pick of what you thought was a simple tab of dry material would draw out with it a deep horrifying oyster of bloody and retchworthy afterthoughts: in school I would have to crouch behind the propped-up top of my desk until I had cleaned myself up. Could Patty know this about me and not begin to mix into her idea of me a faint and increasing contempt for my abject, charmless, filthy stealth? Before we were engaged, Patty once told me that she had had a prophetic dream image of me in ten years, not married to her and unsuccessful as a higher journalist (my publicly expressed ambition), lounging on a brown vinyl couch with a wrinkled Pier 1 throw sliding off it, and wearing an old sweater with "a long hole" in it. She had married me to save me from that future. Later "the length of the hole" evolved to become a shorthand indicator of how bleak or upbeat I felt about the sustainability of my career outside of technical writing, and I was not at all sure that (since in fact I did wear the same clothes repeatedly on days I didn't have to go into work, and had allowed through negligence a summer moth to chew an almost unnoticeable hole in the shoulder of the cable-knit sweater Patty had given me for my birthday) the repulsive disclosure that I had been picking my nose that night one foot from her head might not very well push her idea of me a bit closer to that awful image of me in disappointment and bad-tempered decline. Even if I led into the fact that I had been picking my nose beside her in bed with a full disclosure of my boyhood nasal adventures, including an account of how I had been unable to use normal swear words until I was eighteen (although my parents used "shitty little" and "Christ on a crutch" fairly freely) and had substituted "Muke!" and "highly mucotic" even for "Dammit!" and "crappy," and how at music school I had tested my willpower by trying to hold a ringing tuning fork to my nostril hairs without flinching, surprised at how unbearable even the briefest buzz, evidently setting off an evolved protective reaction against some big flying jungle insect, felt (whereas a stilled tuning fork, both tines inserted about half an inch, was cool and quite musingly pleasant)—even if she would be happy to know these things about me, removed in time, she might still understandably recoil from the idea that she went to bed with and had borne the child of a person who lay in the dark next to her breathing funnily because he was picking his nose. Yet as with the man in the joke who when given a glass of snot to drink drains it dry, and when asked why, says, "What could I do?—it was all one strand," everything in my life seemed to enjamb splicelessly into everything else, and thus it was with considerable effort that I saved the admission of my nose-picking for another night, perhaps after I had done something status-raising, such as write a monograph on the comma, and I whispered instead:

"I was thinking about the history of punctuation. I guess I was repeating sample sentences of prose to myself. That must have been the snuffling you heard."

"What's funny about the history of punctuation?" she asked.

"Nothing."

"Then why are you smiling madly? I can hear popping sounds coming from your gums, you're smiling so hard."

I seized her shoulder. "Remember that time? Remember that time in college when you said, 'Bacon frying'?"

12.

S HE SAID she did remember. It was one of my treasured college
moments. I had been working on "Dickinson's Brain" all evening
and was operatic with caffeine. I brushed my teeth and went into
Patty's dorm room very late—Anita, who had the upper bunk,
slept regularly with someone down the hall—and as I got in bed
next to Patty, who was already asleep, I suddenly thought of
something Jim Heydemann, who was by then in his first year of
medical school, had told me on the phone a week earlier. (I had
fallen behind Jim by taking a year-and-a-half leave from college.)
He had said he was doing an obstetrical rotation, and when I
made some comment about how incredible it was that the human
female vagina could stretch the way it did, he said, with pretend
old-handness, "Eh, sometimes it tears, of course, but as the
resident who's taking us around says, 'Man, you put two pieces of
a vagina in the same *room* together and they'll heal.' " I had told
this to Patty immediately, but she had said that it belittled
women's anatomies and forbade me to share it with her friends in
the cafeteria over dinner. Yet as I lay next to her in her lower bunk,

93

the idea of two wizened but perky pieces of a vagina perched like Agatha Christie characters in opposite corners of a room catching sight of each other and waving and putting their teacups down and eagerly healing their way toward each other seemed funny all over again: I smiled an unusually wide smile in the dark, and Patty, half awakened by the salival sounds my smile produced, murmured: "Bacon frying." And at that instant, as I heard her lovely almost unconscious voice adapt my private smile-crackers to the dream requirement of a breakfast image from her presexual, precollege past (of her mother standing in the middle of the kitchen with her arms crossed and a spatula in one hand, scolding a political figure on the morning news?), I felt suddenly much older, and stunned with happiness and gratitude to be in her bunk bed, and I knew I loved her. And when she heard exactly the same smile from me years later, after her own vagina had slowly and imperfectly healed from the "second-degree tear" the Bug had caused, this shortcut back to the beginning of our life together was too much for me: We were parents now! We were a family! I had to tell her!

"Baby. That snuffling you heard was really me picking my nose."

"Ah! That explains it."

"I wasn't going to tell you because I thought if you knew enough grimy little things about me you would suddenly lose your love for me, but apparently I can't not tell you."

"It seems to me that you've picked your nose around me before."

"Really? But never in the nuptial bed, never just after you've turned out the light, right?"

"Well, try to keep it to a minimum. Now tell me something mysterious and fine about your past that you've never told me before, so I don't go off to sleep thinking of you entirely as a pickanoser."

Every two or three weeks, Patty asked me to tell her something I had never told her before about my past, and often I came up dry, but luckily that night the memory of her saying "Bacon frying" summoned to mind the peanut butter and bacon sandwiches my father used to make for himself on Saturday afternoons. Sometimes, I told her, my father made peanut butter and banana sandwiches, but I had to leave the room when he ate those, because I found the combination—those overripe, bilaterally halved bananas which he repeatedly crushed between the slices of toast to a manageable width as each bite he took forced the far side of his sandwich apart—appalling; but peanut butter and bacon, on the other hand, seemed to me to be an ideal fatherly combination, although I myself stuck to grape jelly. These sandwiches even had a name: he called them "graveyards." My mother cooked the bacon in the morning (it owed its seersucker shrivelment, I thought, to the fact that the meaty striations contracted less than the fatty part, or vice versa: the pinpricks of exploding fat on my forearms and face were part of the brave scientific pleasure of studying the way it changed shape), and she laid it out to cool on paper towels; my sister and I had already eaten our share, but four strips remained on the paper towel for my father long after the grease from the pan was poured into a reused medium-size peanut butter jar on the stove—a peanut butter jar that had been run through the dishwasher enough times that the glue under its label had softened: if you unclamped the dishwasher's lid at the right moment (this was a red-hosed top-loading portable whose hermetic clamped seal was almost as perfect as the one on a brand-new jar of Skippy) and, in a cloud of lovely garbagey-smelling steam, removed the freshly dishwashed jar, you could sometimes slip the now paler and mushier label untorn off the glass like one of the water-mobilized decals that came with the plastic models of fighter planes. In this clean and label-less peanut butter jar my mother recorded the history of each week in grease: unequal strata, some cloudy, some clear, some yellowish, some with a black crumb of hamburger or a tiny miscellaneous chicken bone suspended in them, some with little sketchy depressions left by a shameless mouse whose even bolder descendants years later used to spend whole nights of debauch in the by this time built-in and front-loading dishwasher, climbing around those rubberized jungle gyms when we forgot to shut the door on the dirty dishes. It was obvious to me when I described them to Patty that these sandwiches were called graveyards be-cause the strips of bacon suggested bodies buried in the Nilotic ooze of the peanut butter; but at the time I never speculated on the logic of their name, which, thanks to my father's ability to convey his enthusiasm about everything he ate or did or thought about, I learned early enough for it to seem as perfectly suited to its referent as *broom* or *road* or *envelope*; the exciting thing for me about calling it a graveyard was simply that it was one of the very few sandwiches that wasn't sterilely identified by its principal middle ingredient—the Reuben, the *croque-monsieur*, and the club sandwich being some other examples of an elect order that borrowed its glamour from the bigger-than-life bar carnage of Bloody Marys and Hurricanes. My father spread the peanut butter on the hot toast, using what appeared to be all that was left in the jar—the circling knife and spoon passes visible through the glass made it look like a ball of messily wound twine—but I knew that there was almost always enough to make another sandwich if I used methods of secondary and tertiary recovery, catching the stuff that was left in the center of the jar's base and just below the rim; in covering a whole side of bread from an apparently empty jar I compared myself to the Kalahari Bushmen my mother told me about, who had a use for every part of a felled antelope and ate even the wax in its ear canals. My father tore the cool limp strips of bacon in half and arranged them in a grid and closed the sandwich over them; then he beckoned me with his graveyard into the alcove, where he considered putting on Brahm's Third or Buxtehude's "Absalon, My Son" with its grief-stricken trombones but rejected them in favor of Bach: "Time for some of that *Art of el Fugue-o*! Got to have it!"—and when the bass line entered with the augmented fugue subject we punched its rhythm out in the air with our fists, staring side by side out the window. Between big infrequent bites of his sandwich he showed me how to count off sets of trembling isometric exercises to the music: since he never brought a glass of water or Tang to help wash things down in an emergency, I would worry, when the throat-constricting emotion of an especially beautiful stretto combined with the exertion of the isometrics made him take deep breaths through his nose as he chewed, that he was going to choke; but he waved away my concern. Sometimes when he finished the sandwich he would demonstrate how to handstand to Stravinsky: at sixteen he had been able to hold himself suspended through the whole last side of the Pierre Monteux 78-rpm recording of the *Rite*, collapsing immediately after the last tutti crunch. Now, after I lowered the needle at the beginning of the tumultuously iridescent band of side 2 (of the LA Philharmonic's rendition) that was equivalent to that last Monteux 78, he took off his glasses and assumed a sprinter's crouch amid the album covers and back issues of *Stereo Review*, and at the orchestra's panicky signal he kicked his legs up effortlessly, one first, the other slowly following, making a single grunt more to articulate the moment he achieved poise than to relieve any muscular strain. His body formed a close parenthesis; he stared at his widely planted hands, which at first seemed perfectly still, but showed themselves when you looked longer to be tendonously alive with the precise adjustments of support necessary to keep him steadily upside down. I shouted encouragement over the thumping polytonality; in response, he hopped the fingers of his right hand into a teepee shape and then, canting himself slightly, lifted that hand for a moment from the carpet and held it against his leg. When his left elbow began vibrating under the double load, he went back to the two-hand stance, and this time the shift of his weight suddenly released an outpouring of change and keys and dirty silver stumps of Life Savers that until then had stayed put in his pockets. They lay in two scattered patterns on the rug: a grown man's change, rich with quarters. I had a moment of worry. "Don't go to the end if you don't want to," I shouted: but even over the penultimate brasses I heard his voice, with the curious Peter Lorre tone that upside-downness imposes on the larynx, reply, "Not long now." The piccolo did its final rip, and then the orchestra slammed down. My father allowed his feet to descend slowly to the floor.

"Not quite able to sustain the one-hander," he said, very flushed but low-voiced again and happy with himself. "Woo! Visceral stuff! Now let's see you try." And as my father held my legs in the air, Stravinsky began his slow, aged-man's ascent up an endless flight of stairs in the last spiral of the vinyl, a spiral I thought of as merely the two-dimensional equivalent of the molded glass screw threads over which the lid slid and sealed on a jar of peanut butter.

13.

Rocking, I was impressed by the tenuity of the vacuum (or, as members of the Royal Society once proudly called it, the *vacuum Boylianum*) that the Bug was able to create in her bottle. Because I was wearing the birthday sweater, and I didn't want evaporated milk to drip onto my sleeve as it normally did, I had given the nipple-holder an extra turn today; this unusually tight fit made it a little harder for air to file in with its faint squealing cries along the bottle's plastic screw threads and take its place in neat semicircular bubble-rows in the interior, substituting for the liquid the Bug had most recently swallowed. Only a warm ounce or two remained. Shadows were shifting in the cheese grater. The rocking chair still preserved its textural silence over the floorboards, a silence embowered rather than corrupted by the minuscule whizzing coming from the bottle and the soft hums of the Bug's breathing, and the Mr.-Softee-truck-style pre-recorded church bells that occasionally rang in a steeple several miles away, and the distant bowling-ball sounds reaching us from one of the six or seven planes that if I leaned a bit to the right I could have spotted under one windowshade far across sunlit Quincy Bay landing and taking off against the Boston horizon (a low mound of glass now the late-afternoon color of thermally activated elevator call buttons) as smoothly and deliberately as long passes of the four-story Foucault pendulum in the Franklin Institute, where Patty and I went during pre-exam reading period one semester and I experienced a moment of claustrophobic panic as we toured the lacquered, thumping ventricles of the walk-through human heart on the second floor. A crowd of excited schoolkids pressed behind us; I moved forward and downward into the heart's warmer substandard air, crouching to avoid bonking my head on various myocardial constrictions in the passageway; Patty (ahead of me because I didn't want my already visible bald spot bobbing in front of her the whole time) led me up and down narrowing stairways and U turns past signs saying "Right Ventricle" and "Septum" as my own merely life-size utensil began to outpace the endlessly looping tape-recording pumped through the exhibit's walls from some enormous central woofer; once she turned and, seeing my half-joking scared stare, took my hand and shouted, "We're almost through—I see light!" But, as in those teasing false exits into second-floor daylight in midway haunted houses, we shuffled past a brief catwalk glimpse of the rest of the biotechnology exhibit and then, as the arterial tunnel closed over us again and the thronging schoolchildren raised a jubilant racket, we veered and plunged steeply down past a sign that unexpectedly announced: *You are now entering the Lungs.* And here I felt a spasm of true panic which made me grip Patty's ribs and draw close to her and try roughly to sniff in any cool outdoor oxygen that might have remained undisturbed deep in the thick insulation of her nape hair, stepping unintentionally on the heel of her tennis shoe as I did so (something she told me

was known on the playground as "giving somebody a flat tire"),
a panic that disappeared completely the moment we finally
clumped out the aortal exit but which I artificially sustained and
exaggerated as we flaggingly toured the other floors ("Gee, my
heart is *still going!*"), wanting perhaps to give her a special reason
to love me, a tender extracurricular vulnerability unwittingly
revealed, and also perhaps curious as to what her techniques of
comforting were like—and when we sat on a bench near the
elevator and she said, "There, there, there, baby—that human
heart gave you a bad scare, a bad, bad scare," in time-honored
soothing cadences, I whimpered happily, "It did! It really did!"

The Bug experienced a similar panic when I dressed her clum-
sily: as soon as she felt the neckhole of a pullover widening
resistingly, like Patty's cervix, over her head, she thought she was
being suffocated, and thrashed and cried; recently I had begun
stretching out all the neckholes ruthlessly before trying to get her
through them, and I even attempted to prop them open with my
splayed fingers and thumbs, so that the fabric would not graze her
face and trigger the claustrophobia, as I had learned to do long
before with my own underpants after a shower, holding each
leghole very wide, as if it were a figure in a game of cat's cradle, so
that none of the possible loathsome tile-slimes on my feet could
make contact with fabric that would be hugging my organs of
reproduction all day, since what was the point of fresh underwear
if it was aglow with athlete's foot even before it had reached its
destination? Thirty years of such little masteries could now find
new twists and applications in fatherhood. I held nothing back for
her! I loved her! When I first read Nabokov's *Glory*, I had been
bothered by a sentence early on that claimed that the mother's
love for the hero was so violent and intense "that it seemed to
make the heart hoarse." Basic anatomy aside, the phrase seemed

wrong—strained and conventional and rhythmically bad and untrue to the real sensations of love. I ascribed its general inadequacy to some especially tricky problem of translation. But now that I had the Bug to care for three days a week, I noticed that this phrase, which I had remembered only as something puzzlingly out of character, was coming to mind increasingly frequently, and seeming each time to capture more exactly the real pneumatics of the parental sensation: sometimes in looking at the Bug I felt as if I was crumpling up, hunching my shoulders, deflating like a poolside flotation toy to be folded away for the winter—the same collapsing feeling that Mal Green had induced by forcing me to play the Chiarnovsky in one breath: not the vocal hoarseness of prolonged shouting or whispering or even of talking for hours on a long car trip, but the deeper lungier expiration of blowing up a balloon (especially on an empty stomach), and transferring your pneuma to it. My mother, who I think loved my sister and me to the point of heart-hoarseness, taught us how to make clay coin banks by blowing up and tying balloons and then wrapping them in gray clay: we pinched the surfaces of the clay-covered balloons into guinea pigs or owls or bullfrogs (one of the teaching assistants did a nice caricatured head of my mother), but as we worked we were still able to sense the poppable resilience of the pale spheres underneath. And then coin slots were carefully cut and the clay banks were allowed to dry and fired to an off-white gritty color in a kiln: and our selfless balloons within were—my mother taught us the word—"vaporized" in thousands of degrees of heat: I shook my heavy frog bank and heard a slight dead-light-bulb tinkle—crumbs no doubt of the vanished but heroic balloon (of the bunchier, tied navel part that always tended downward when the balloon was aloft?), which had been consumed, along with our hoarse inflating breaths, in order to maintain the essential hollowness around which an animal likeness was only decoration, a hollowness I slowly filled with coins I found in the cool depths of the blue couch or under the seat of the car or on the alcove rug near the stereo albums, and then restored once again by sliding the change coin by coin out of the slot with the blade of a butter knife, as a baby-sitter showed us, in order to buy Christmas presents, and then filled up again. But this time I was too impatient to knife each coin out and instead shattered the bank on the driveway and counted the money and found that I was forty-eight cents short of being able to buy the two plastic models I wanted to hybridize—a Corvette funny car and a Flying Fortress. In a trance of nine-year-old wrongdoing, I opened my mother's pocketbook, with its attractive hinges, and found her small blue leather change purse, held shut by a beautiful simple pair of gold projections whose decorous bulbousness I much later came to associate with the clitoris, but whose smooth solution of the problem of purse closure seemed even then wonderfully unlocksmithied, unstrongboxlike, and therefore feminine, and I stole two cold quarters and hid each under a corner of an Oriental rug and waited for her to come in from the kitchen. "I think I'll look for some more money," I said, when she did appear. "I haven't looked under this rug, I don't think. No, nothing there. What about this rug? Oh! A quarter. Wow, a whole quarter!" My fingers trembled. I was unable to pretend, as I had planned, to look casually under radiators and on windowsills to develop the necessary context of fortuity; I went directly to the other rug's corner and flipped it back as well. "And here's another one!" My mother looked mildly surprised.

As I was rushing off with my paper bag of money to the drugstore where the plastic models were sold, I ran into her standing in the driveway, with her pocketbook open on the hot hood of the car. She had been on her way to teach an art class, I think, and was planning to buy cigarettes on the way. I had never seen her look so imploringly miserable. She asked if I had taken the quarters from her purse. I ordered my neck muscles to shake my head.

"Okay," she said. "I believe you." She got in the car.

With the help of the stolen quarters, I bought the two models and built the hybrid with Jim Heydemann, but we were more careless with the dollops of glue than usual and got fingerprints on the fuselage and grew dissatisfied with it, and together we baked it in a slow oven until its wings drooped and its propellers looked as if they had been drawn by Dr. Seuss; and then, near the garbage cans, we lit two molded GIs in fighting stance and fused them onto each wing, aflame and out of scale, and as burning drops of plastic fell onto the driveway with an odd purring sound (caused by the air overfeeding and frictionally suppressing the flame at the same time), we crashed the ruined Corvette-airplane—Prestone decals and all—against the foundation of the house, making cries of agony, and then doused it with a squirt gun and threw it away. And perhaps if my mother hadn't discovered the theft of the quarters and said so terrifyingly that she believed me, I would never have had the fortitude to tell Patty the truth about picking my nose that night.

.... .14. ....

THE VACUUM IN THE BOTTLE had gotten powerful enough now to be interfering with the further delivery of milk, so I gently pulled its nipple from the Bug's mouth. With her eyes closed, she struggled to prevent this detachment, lifting her head a little way off my arm, but as soon as the tip of her tongue parted from the nipple's crosshatch, breaking the seal, and air seethed in rapidly, she smiled a big loopy smile, like a rubber band in midflight, at the unexpectedly reciprocal respiration. Her eyes stayed closed. Her lips were swollen from sucking: as she waited, openmouthed, for me to reinstate the nipple, I spotted her pulse beating in her lower lip—in her *lip!*—something I had never seen before, or known was a thing people could ever see, or would want to see. I gave her back the bottle; she made six or seven automatic sucking pulls at it and then let her mouth go slack again: she was asleep. I smiled back at her, amazed at her beauty—amazed at her caterpillar eyelashes and her clean nose and the reposeful thoughtless angles of her clean pale hair and at the red heartbeat visible for the first time in her lower lip—but a moment after this familiar rapture passed I was puzzled: when I had smiled adoringly just then, and when the Bug had smiled in her sleep a second earlier, our mouths had not made the bacon-frying sounds that Patty had heard those two happy times next to me in bed, once in college and once recently. Experimentally, I made a big Stevie Wonder face, and then I tried a few even wider, dental-instrument grimaces, and I confirmed that I could not now reproduce the popping sounds that had so clearly been audible to Patty. It was not, I didn't think, that the quality of my emotion caused a physically distinct type of smile, although of course a smile of admiration for the Bug's beauty was not identical in its musculature to a caffeinacious smile in the dark at a forbidden statement about healing vaginas, or to an abased but imminently truth-telling you-caught-me-picking-my-nose expression. No, the explanation had to be that smiles became audible only at bedtime because *toothpaste altered the chemical characteristics of one's saliva in a way that encouraged an unusually loud, sticky effervescence along the gum line.* And think—this smile sound was just one of many mouth sounds the Bug was going to notice and master in time! Speech was one, of course—but also the loud woodblock tock we learned in second grade, made by cupping the tongue muscle under the roof of the mouth like a chiton and pulling it down while holding the lips in an amplifying O; or the interesting ducklike squirts you could make by enclosing two pillows of air high in the cheeks, just below the cheekbones, and then forcing these reserves to surge forward into the nameless tissues above the front teeth; or the plinks and squeaks of a rubber band stretched tightly through the lower dentition and plucked by the tongue until the cheddar-cheese pain of the rubber band's edge against your gums made your eyes water and you pulled the loop free and again stretched it over the

porcelain knobs of your dresser and let the spit fling itself heed-
lessly off in vibration; or the little kissy noise you could make by
sucking the air from the blue cap of a Bic pen and letting it seal
itself against your tongue and after you'd waggled it thoughtfully
for a while pulling it free; or the much more substantial steel-
drum effect you got by plucking your tongue free of the vacuum it
had effortfully hauled from a soft-drink bottle before the gas
escaping from the remaining soda negated your work; or the
superb though eventually painful waterdrop *poips* that a trumpet
player named Dan taught many of us brass instrumentalists at
Eastman, in which you flicked your fingernail against the outside
of one cheek while pushing out a whistle with your tongue: the
percussion of the fingernail added a cavernous depth and rotun-
dity to the sound that Wordsworth must have had in mind when
he wrote the nice line in *The Prelude* about the ruined roofless
cathedral whose

shuddering ivy dripped large drops.

Already the Bug had mastered a gentler, more clucking version of
my second-grade playground-clearing chiton tock: I made the
noise in slow motion for her one morning while she stared up at
me from the changing table, and, surprising herself, she clucked
softly back. Godspeed! She was on her way! Soon enough she
would feel the privileged relation with the audible world that
comes after playing with a toy tape recorder; and this reifying
severance of sound from source would be reinforced as she fell
under the sway of the triple-personification of the commonplace
noise that an oven-toasted rice cereal made as it deliquesced in
milk, and young Snap and his clean-living companions took their
place of primacy before Gluttony, Orgoglio, Boreas, Sin, Death,

Enitharmon, the Invisible Hand, and all the rest of the shadowy parade of older allegorical figures; and she would jump just as my father had and I now did every time a telephone rang on a TV show just as I began to doze off, tricked repeatedly by the concentrated tinny realism of the noise in the midst of some utterly unrealistic convention-ridden crime drama—no doubt the same especially fine telephone-ring was overdubbed show after show, year after year, long after the telephone itself had been reconditioned and resold to a couple with a new baby living in an apartment on Wollaston Hill.

But there was one sound she might never know as I had known it. In my second and last semester at Eastman, boy did I feel I was doing something original and thrilling when, inspired by Debussy's advice to listen only to the wind that in passing recounts the history of the world, and by his neat dismissal of a section of a Witkowski symphony as "a laboratory devoted to the study of vacuums," I decided after reading his biography to begin my first symphonic piece with the implosive atmospheric instauration of a newly opened jar of peanut butter. Of course the percussion section would be entrusted with the carrying out of this novelty, just as they had been the ones to master and legitimize the exotic *cymbales antiques* that Debussy himself had introduced into orchestration. I imagined the premiere in St. Louis or Pittsburgh: the solemn nod from the conductor, the jar of Skippy Creamy held high, label outward, yet close enough to the surreptitious microphone that no detail of its first breath would be lost: the moment of topcoated strain, the moment of soundless lid-turning, and then the humble *fup* of the sound itself: sound made from the sudden arrival of the possibility of sound, circular thunder. Was it program music? Only in the sense (as I would have to explain at defensive length in the program notes) that the daintily vortical second movement of *La Mer* was program music: and indeed the sound of the air entering the peanut butter jar was meant lovingly to sum up Debussy's lifelong fascination with air—his interest in a technique of piano pedaling that would approximate breathing; his wish for a music whose harmonic progressions, although they might sound stifled in the concert hall, would once out of doors enter into a collaboration with the open air and float joyfully over the tops of the trees; his piano preludes, whose titles ("Voiles," "Le Vent dans la plaine," " 'Les sons et les parfums tournent dans l'air du soir,' " "Ce qu'a vu le vent d'ouest," "Brouillards," and so on) repeatedly made aerial references; the recollections by Gabriel Pierné and Camille Bellaigue that his piano technique was accompanied by his "puffing noisily during the difficult passages" and by "a kind of hiccup or harsh puff" to mark the beginning of every bar.

I worried that the audience wouldn't have time to get all this if the jar opened too readily, and therefore I hoped that the percussionist would by chance encounter one of those infrequent Peter Pans or Skippy Creamies that was the product of an improperly calibrated piece of screwing machinery, so that as he struggled covertly to turn the lid, increasingly embarrassed and frustrated, his jaw clenched, his fiercely whispered "You little piece of shit!" sizzling from the loudspeaker horns, his membership in the musicians' union suddenly open to doubt, and as he fussily excused himself to go backstage and run the jar under hot water for a minute, we all might use that lucky delay to think of the meteorological greatness stored and quality-sealed in *La Mer*, or, more likely, of times when we had undergone similar failures with jars of peanut butter (or jelly or spaghetti sauce)—when we, or I at least, determined to succeed on a third attempt, pretwisted my hands and allowed the drumstick of thumb flesh on my right hand to settle over the slight tractive fluting on the edge of the lid, while the fingers of this same hand curled and clamped to its curvature, all of them leaning to one side, as a row of knees in a concert hall will all lean to accommodate a late-arriving ticket holder. Staring straight ahead, I began the twist itself: I exerted force; then greater force; then folded myself around the jar, and, shaking with extreme effort, blood booming in my eardrums, hooting spittle, gave it my personal best, hunching with it past my crotch to my knees. And I failed. I opened the palm of my pained lid-hand: in its valley I saw a long, white, warming zipper mark of defeat. So I took the jar into the alcove and gave it wordlessly to my father, who loved being sought out with impossible packaging. He stood tall, gripping the jar and looking sideways, invincibly infused with high-volume Bach, and pursed his lips once in concentrated struggle; but when, almost immediately, he felt the lid beginning to move, he instinctively slacked off on his torque, wanting in the foreknowledge of success to prolong the brief but fine interval before the vacuum was breached, in which the downward curve of his own exertion and the slow start-up of lid motion passed through a momentary equilibrium, and the jar seemed to be unscrewing smoothly under its own power. Once the air finally thumped its humid confirmation, he kindly retightened the lid and handed the vessel back for me to open again by myself.

All this, I had thought, would be right there in the first note of my first symphony. If the idea was possibly a bit close to the beginning of *The Lawrence Welk Show*—the popping cork and drifting bubbles—so what! I was inverting that geriatric celebration: attaining air pressure, rather than releasing it; aligning myself and my peanut butter jar with unchampagneworthy domestic exhaustion-machines like medicine droppers, suction darts, toilet plungers, light bulbs, turkey basters, TV screens, vacuum cleaners, breast pumps, thermoses, and vacuum tubes and their vanished drugstore testing kiosks. And if my symphony proved popular and entered the standard repertoire, the orchestra managers would, like champagne stewards themselves, have to lay in case after case of peanut butter (since each performance would demand a brand-new jar), so that even when it came to be packaged in new ways, or possibly was no longer eaten at all, my work could still be performed "with original instrumentation."

.... .15. . . . .

IN HER SLEEP, the Bug made one last communication: a long hiccupy inward breath, a sob played backward, the last remaining evidence of a burst of tearful bad temper half an hour before. A full day with the Bug had so many highs and lows, all forgotten almost immediately, that when these soft suspirative afterimages of unhappiness returned, as now, I had to think back carefully to remember what specifically she had been crying about—in this case it had been some inarticulate frustration with the inflatable globe, which tended to roll away from her hands when she tried to take hold of it. But as I located the Bug's earlier unhappiness I also remembered something else: a mezzo-soprano in my theory class at Eastman with a very hearty rich laugh, but a laugh whose component "hahs" of mirth, if removed from the many "hah-hahs" on either side of them in the descending series, would have sounded like wails of inconsolable remorse; and I felt a surge of pity toward this mezzo-soprano (though I had not really known her and had no idea what she was doing now—probably being successful in some small opera company), because her laugh represented what I now thought life was like for people who were single and without a family. I felt a huge near-miss sort of relief, not quite complacence yet but approaching it, to be established, with an apartment, with this Bug in my arms, with this sweater on and wife who had picked it out, and I felt that though I had not proven to be a composer or a horn player, and was in fact making an unimpressive living as a part-time technical writer and reviewer of TV commercials, and would never write a scholarly history of the comma, I was nonetheless doing all right. Of course I had never finished the symphonic poem that was to begin with the peanut butter jar—I never even got beyond noting that first accented quarter note halfway down a blank piece of music paper, below the tuba line and above the strings (a quarter note without the normal oval bulb at the end but rather the X that in percussion scoring sometimes indicates pitchless indeterminacy, and recalls too the Xs that once stood for eyes in newspaper cartoons of dead people and rag dolls), and it was true that ever since I had transferred from Eastman and my musical proficiencies and ambitions had faded, and I had stopped listening to Debussy and carrying a tuning fork around in my shirt pocket in order to make random objects amplify its unworldly A, my life, like the flaring sheet of water that once in a while will unexpectedly fly up out of the sink if, as you are rinsing some dishes, you allow the tap's strong singular flow to fall accidentally onto a spoon licked clean and left there earlier so that the water is U-turned without an appreciable diminution of force by that single small soffit—that my life, my energies, colliding with the silver spoon of overindulged distraction, had sent me since then in a spray of dissipative directions. Nor had I managed to save even one unopened peanut butter jar; and as I had feared, the packaging was changing: glass was being replaced by plastic, metal lids by plastic lids, and foil inner seals were appearing, like the ones on jars of instant coffee. The Bug would never hear what the glass ones sounded like on opening. The ⅓- and ½- and ¾-cup markings were gone as well: perhaps it was thought to be an insult to the homemaker to imply that he or she would have to stoop to reusing an old peanut butter jar to measure the quantities in a fancy recipe. But fortunately, obeying some warning sense of their endangeredness, I had dishwashed and kept one of the Skippy jars that Patty had spooned from during her pregnancy: it was on my bureau, and it held an assortment of dusty not-quite-pencils that I had no other place for: a Don Diego cigar in an aluminum case, a leftover Slim Jim, a pocket tire-pressure gauge, a thermometer, the magnifying glass that had come in the little drawer of the case for the OED that I had gotten by joining the Book-of-the-Month Club, my tuning fork, the triangular file with three different roughnesses that I had used to file the flashing off pieces of model airplanes before I glued them together, scissors, a machine with a curved blade that clipped articles from newspapers, a six-inch metal pocket ruler with a pocket clip and inches divided into sixty-fourths, some felt-tip pens I'd bought in a rubber-banded bundle in Chinatown for a dollar with the names of distant businesses (Powderhorn Coal Company, Charon Transport) printed on them, a fiberglass conductor's baton, a clay-modeling tool, a dirty feather. The jar was purely decorative: I couldn't use anything in it because any removal was likely to upset the balance of heavy and light objects and cause it to overturn. There was some loose change and a few rubber bands, including the thick red ones that had held together fat stalks of broccoli, in the bottom. Even the Bic pen that I had used to write my senior paper on the word "brain" in Emily Dickinson was stored here: its cap and blue terminal plug were long gone, and it was cracked and white at the end from hours of

continuous chewing, so that its surface resembled the indoor ice
that the smiley figure skater had skated and spun on so roughly
with the identical model of Bic pen strapped to her heel in one of
the "Writes first time, every time" ads: I would have had only to
chew it for three or four minutes now for my cuspids to reawaken
that nice almost chocolatey or anise-like headache-inducing taste
of resinous clear plastic, a taste similar to the mentholyptal air in
sun-warmed inflatable toys as you forced in a few last tightening
breaths, or the taste of a hot sharp squirt from a squirt gun when
you triggered it against the roof of your mouth after the glinting
green toy was rediscovered lying on the porch steps late in the
afternoon—a sensation that must, I thought, have something in
common with sucking milk from a plastic bottle. A few times,
Patty had let me watch her pump milk from her gigundo breasts
before she left for work, using the clear plastic Gentle Expressions
manual breast pump: off-white flaxen threads, much finer than a
squirt gun's output, were drawn at odd angles from here and there
on her vacuum-leavened nipple, in a suction not nearly as effi-
cient as that induced by the Bug's mouth: after ten minutes of
pumping, there would have accumulated enough milk in the
transparent canister to fill one corner of a plastic bag, and later I
would defrost one of these twist-tied quartz pillows of nutrition
and squeeze it into a slush and warm it in a bowl and try to feed
the Bug with it before her nap, until the whole sequence began to
seem crazily time-consuming and we switched to Carnation
evaporated, despite the pediatrician's firm preference for formula,
which the Bug refused. And if in ten years Bic pens were still
around, and the Bug, inconceivably long-limbed, were to chew
on one as she sat in class writing about birds or airplanes or the
virtues of garbagemen, making large careful commas, she might
taste the same quizzical six-sided plastic taste and wonder why it

tasted so good and so awful at the same time—so addictively sickening—and why the sound of her saliva fizzing through the tiny airhole in the side of the pen's barrel was such a peculiarly satisfying, calming, thought-provoking sound, and if she brought the chewed pen home, I could explain that it might have something to do with the hint of plastic in the warm evaporated milk that Patty and I had fed her from a six-sided bottle on magnificent fall afternoons when she was a tiny baby, only six months old. Everything in my life was beginning to route itself through the Bug. I carried her to her crib and zipped her up in her flame-retardant incunabulum: she shook her head twice when she felt the withdrawal of my hands under her, but she stayed asleep. I gazed at her idolatrously. Over her head, the inspection slips fluttered for a few seconds to mark her airborne passage and then grew still. I picked up the TLS from next to the rocking chair and tiptoed out of the room with it.